Ripple *Of* Secrets

A ROSE GARDNER NOVELLA

BETWEEN THIRTY-THREE AND THIRTY-FOUR

Other books by Denise Grover Swank:

Rose Gardner Mysteries
(Humorous Southern mysteries)
TWENTY-EIGHT AND A HALF WISHES
TWENTY-NINE AND A HALF REASONS
THIRTY AND A HALF EXCUSES
FALLING TO PIECES (novella)
THIRTY-ONE AND A HALF REGRETS
THIRTY-TWO AND A HALF COMPLICATIONS
PICKING UP THE PIECES (novella)
THIRTY-THREE AND A HALF SHENANIGANS
THIRTY-FOUR AND A HALF PREDICAMENTS

The Wedding Pact
(Rom-Com)
THE SUBSTITUTE

Chosen Series
(Urban fantasy)
CHOSEN
HUNTED
SACRIFICE
REDEMPTION

On the Otherside Series
(Young adult science fiction/romance)
HERE
THERE

Curse Keepers
(Adult urban fantasy)
THE CURSE KEEPERS
THE CURSE BREAKERS
THE CURSE DEFIERS

Off the Subject
(New Adult Contemporary Romance)
AFTER MATH
REDESIGNED
BUSINESS AS USUAL

Ripple

Of

Secrets

A ROSE GARDNER NOVELLA
BETWEEN THIRTY-THREE AND THIRTY-FOUR

Denise Grover Swank

This book is a work of fiction. References to real people, events, establishments, organizations, or locations are intended only to provide a sense of authenticity, and are used fictitiously. All other characters, and all incidents and dialogue, are drawn from the author's imagination and are not to be construed as real.

Cover art and design: Eisley Jacobs
Developmental Editor: Angela Polidoro
Copy editor: Shannon Page
Proofreaders: Leigh Morgan

ISBN- 978-1507859759

Chapter One
Joe

My parents' house was the last place I wanted to be on Christmas Day.

Coming home for just the day had become a tradition after I started law school in Little Rock. It fulfilled my family obligation without forcing me to spend any more time with my parents than necessary. Even before my entire life fell apart back in September, I'd hoped to get out of going to my parents' house for Christmas. Only I'd hoped to be spending Christmas with Rose, planning our wedding and our family, our life together. Now my future seemed as barren as the gray day outside my car.

As I drove through the open gate, I considered pulling around the circular drive and taking off, but I knew it was just a fantasy. Still, I was grateful to find the brick-paved drive surprisingly empty. My parents usually threw elaborate Christmas parties. They must have still been too humiliated by my state senate loss to host one this year. Especially one I would be attending.

I parked close to the front door, then gripped the steering wheel and took a deep breath as I stared at the massive brick and stone house. Thank God for my sheriff patrol shift later. I'd volunteered to fill in for one of the deputies with a family so he could spend the entire day with his kids. I would have pulled a double shift if I could have gotten away with it, but my father had made some vague threat about "that Fenton County tart" and I'd mumbled that I'd figure out a way to come.

Rose and I might not be together, but I would gladly spend the rest of my life keeping her safe, whether she knew it or not. It was my penance for failing her.

A lump filled my throat, catching me by surprise. My good days outnumbered my bad ones lately, but the holidays had been rough. I'd purposely tried to avoid Rose over the last week, a difficult task given the fact that we were now business partners. But that was no one's fault but my own. My last-ditch effort to keep her in my life. While I'd gone into it knowing her initial outrage would soften, I'd hoped her resistance to taking me back would fade as well. But her relationship with Mason seemed stronger than ever, especially after Mason's brush with death in the fire at that strip club Gems. It was all I could do to block out the mental image of the two of them celebrating Christmas at Rose's farmhouse.

That was supposed to be me.

But it was time to suck it up and accept the situation. At least for now. I still held out hope. Things changed. The crash course of our relationship was proof enough of that. Rose had told me she wanted safe instead of risky for now. She had been talking about the business, of course, but the look in her eyes had given me hope that her words might hold a double meaning. I'd bide my time. Rose was worth waiting for.

I squared my shoulders and climbed out of the car, grateful the forecasted rain had held off and the sun was peeking through the clouds. It bolstered my resolve as I knocked on the front door and waited. My parents' butler, Gerald, opened the door moments later, a grim look on his face.

"Cheer up, Gerald," I said, brushing past him as I walked through the door. "It's Christmas and my parents don't seem to be having their usual boisterous party."

Gerald's only response was to close the door behind me. He'd worked for my parents for nearly twenty years and truth be told, I couldn't remember Gerald ever looking happy. But then again, look where he worked.

The entryway was covered with Christmas decorations. Real evergreen garland was wrapped around the staircase railing, as well as an elaborate holiday arrangement on the mahogany credenza. The image was worthy of a magazine layout. In fact, it had probably been featured in one. My parents were known for their multiple holiday parties and my mother hired a decorator every year. It took the decorator days to make the house visually ready for Christmas. But no matter how perfect it looked, there was always something missing—something only I seemed to notice. Heart and love. The setting was as soulless as it was beautiful.

Just like the woman who claimed to be carrying my child.

My parents were already sitting in the living room. My mother was dressed to impress in a cream-colored suit that blended in strategically with the off-white sofa, sipping a mimosa from a champagne flute. Dad was in an overstuffed chair, drinking coffee while reading a newspaper.

Mom noticed me first, her gaze lifting to my face. A soft smile lifted her mouth and I had a hard time figuring out if it was genuine or if she thought it was expected of her. Maybe both.

She kicked into hostess mode, even if it was only a party of three. "Joe, how lovely for you to join us."

I considered adding that I hadn't had a choice in the matter, but we all knew it and I would come across as a sulking child. "Merry Christmas, Mom." I tried hard to keep the sarcasm from my voice.

Dad barely glanced up at me. "Joseph."

I was tempted to pay a visit to the wet bar in the corner, but I'd done a lot of soul-searching lately, and I realized I'd used alcohol as a crutch for too long. Instead, I sat on the opposite end of the sofa from my mother. It occurred to me that while it was a relief my parents hadn't included their usual guests, it also meant there was no one else present to distract them.

"How's your new job?" Mom asked, the disgust in her voice only partially veiled.

"It's going great, thanks for asking." The sarcasm in my own voice was far more obvious.

"Are you really moving to that *farm?*" The way she said 'farm' made it sound like I was moving to third-world Africa.

"Yes, I'm moving this week, actually."

Her upper lip curled. "I don't understand why you don't move in with Hilary. She's leased such a lovely house, a rare find in that dump of a town."

"For the hundredth time, I'm not moving in with Hilary. And I'm definitely not marrying her."

"She's carrying your child, Joseph." Her voice sounded strained.

My father looked up, as if finally taking notice of our conversation. "You will not make that child a bastard, Joseph."

My hand balled into a fist. "This is the twenty-first century, Dad."

He set his paper down in his lap and narrowed his eyes. "That child will be a Simmons. I will see to it."

"J.R.," an all-too-familiar voice cooed from across the room. "No need for threats."

My chest tightened as I glanced at the woman in the doorway. "You invited Hilary?"

She stood in the threshold wearing a gray linen skirt paired with a white silk blouse that revealed her growing cleavage, but she'd dressed down the outfit with two-inch heels instead of her usual three or four. Her long red hair was loose today and her makeup was understated. Hilary was a beautiful woman and she knew it. In fact, she relied on it. This morning it was obvious she was going for a Christmas casual look, only it looked plastic on her. I couldn't help but wonder what Rose was wearing.

"Of course we invited Hilary," Mom said as though I'd asked the stupidest question in the world. "She's the mother of your child. She'll be with us *every* Christmas."

My father's eyes found mine and his jaw clenched. "Our grandchildren will spend Christmas at *our* house every year."

If Rose and I ever had children together, I would sooner throw myself on a grenade than bring them here. Why was I so apathetic about the child Hilary was carrying? I might not like the baby's mother, but he or she would still be mine. I needed to accept that and do my level best to protect him or her from these narcissists.

"*Of course* our baby will spend Christmas here," Hilary said, moving to the wet bar. "Don't be ridiculous." She poured herself a glass of orange juice and sat down on the sofa between my mother and me.

I expected her to put her hand on my knee or drape herself against my arm, but she kept her body parts to herself, unlike her usual modus operandi. Hilary had used sex as a way to sway me since we were teenagers. So she was changing tactics. Again. Whatever her plan, she took a sip of her juice and turned to my mother. "My parents called and said they were going to be a few minutes late."

I wasn't surprised to hear that her parents were coming too. This was probably all planned weeks ago. The five of them would gang up on me and try to wear me down. I glanced at the grandfather clock in the entryway. Five minutes down. Three hours and fifty-five minutes to go.

"Hilary, dear, how have you been feeling?" Mom asked her with more warmth than she'd used for me.

"Surprisingly well. Very little morning sickness." She paused for dramatic effect and gave my mother a soft smile. "I'm just exhausted all the time." She released a pretty laugh. "I find myself falling asleep at *ridiculous* times. Just this Wednesday I fell asleep at eight o'clock, if you'd believe it."

My mother grabbed her hand. "You should come back home, Hilary. Let your mother and me take care of you."

My irritation had begun to grate away at my control. "Hilary is a healthy, grown woman. She's not working, and she lives in one of the nicest homes in Henryetta, Arkansas. Pregnancy is not a disease, Mother—she'll be just fine. In fact, Neely Kate Colson is having a much more difficult pregnancy, and the last thing she does is sit around while other people wait on her." I turned to face them both, growing angrier by the minute. "Just last week, she and Rose helped find Neely Kate's missing cousin."

A condescending gleam filled my mother's eyes. "Are you seriously comparing our sweet, delicate Hilary to the Fenton County riffraff?"

I stood, clenching my fists at my sides. "And which one of those women are you calling riffraff, Mother?"

Her face softened and she nodded her head, acting as if I were an upset child who could easily be managed if the right sweets were promised. "Joseph, all of this fuss is unnecessary. If you want to be the chief deputy sheriff in that backwoods county, fine. Do it. Your father thinks your new position will aid you politically more than being with the state police would." She set her champagne flute on the side table, then placed her hands on her knees in a graceful swoop. "But at least have the sense to marry the mother of your child."

"No, Mom." I kept my voice down, but my anger was unmistakable. "You may think you can dictate everything else in my life, but you can *not* make me marry this woman."

My mother and I glared at each other for several long seconds before I heard a woman's voice say, "Well, it's about damn time."

I spun around, my mouth parting as relief washed through me when I saw my younger sister Kate standing in the doorway. I hadn't seen her in a couple of years, but she looked exactly the same except that the red streaks in her short dark bob had been replaced with blue ones. She wore jeans and a long-sleeved gray T-shirt, her thumbs hooked through holes at the ends of the sleeves. Her style was grunge-casual, and I could feel my mother's skin crawl from three feet away. I would have run to her and pulled her into a hug if she hadn't told me to go to hell the last time we'd seen each other, especially since she'd really meant it. But after what had happened, with a couple of years' distance and a bit of maturity on my part, I couldn't say I blamed her.

"Katherine." Disdain dripped off my mother's tongue. "I had no idea you planned to join us for the holidays."

"I heard changes were afoot." She winked at me and glided into the room, perching on the arm of the empty armchair. "I had to see if it was true."

Mom's back stiffened. "Joe and Hilary are expecting a baby, and we're trying to set a wedding date."

"It sounds like you and Hil-Monster are the only two who are concerned with that task." Kate gave Hilary a devilish look and tsked. "Now, now, Hils. The last person I expected to be an unwed mother is you." She got up, headed to the wet bar, and picked up a crystal glass. Clutching it to her chest, she turned to face the couch.

"You must be either getting sloppy or desperate. Personally, I'm going with the latter."

I released a chuckle, but Hilary gasped.

"Katherine," Mom admonished. "Hilary is our guest and you will speak to her with respect."

Kate poured whiskey into her glass. "Guest? Hell, she's practically lived here her entire life." She set the decanter down on the table with a heavy thud and picked up her glass. "She's more like a sister than a guest." She turned her cold eyes on me. "Wouldn't you say so, Joe?" Then she lifted the glass and took a sip. "But if she's really pregnant with your baby, that would be incest."

I cringed. Kate may have viewed Hilary as a sister, but I never had. Maybe it was because even when I was a little boy I'd felt the unspoken expectation that I'd end up with Hilary one day.

"Katherine Elizabeth!" our father shouted. "That will be enough."

Kate seemed unfazed. "Enough what? Honesty?" She walked closer to my father. "I disagree. There never was enough honesty in this house."

My mother shifted in her seat. "Did you come back here to insult us, Katherine? If so, an e-mail would have sufficed."

Kate resumed her seat on the arm of the chair. "No. It's like I told you. I came back to see if Joe really grew a pair of balls." Though she'd addressed our mother, she'd said it while looking at me.

I should have been insulted, but I snickered instead, earning a glare from Hilary.

"If you insist on speaking so coarsely, we will have to insist that you eat Christmas dinner somewhere else," my father said in a tone that suggested he wouldn't tolerate any nonsense.

Too bad it never worked with Kate.

She took a sip of her drink and laughed. "And what exactly are you going to do? Call the police and have me kicked out?" She covered her mouth with the tips of her fingers and released a fake gasp. "And besmirch the Simmons name?" Grinning, she dropped her hand. "No, I don't think so." She tilted her head toward the doorway. "You could try to have Gerald haul me out, but I'm pretty sure I can take 'im."

I burst out laughing. "Things have been dull without you." And while my words were true, I also didn't trust her motives. I believed she was curious, but there had to be more to it. Kate only did things that benefited Kate.

Merriment filled her eyes and she winked. "Glad you grew a pair, big brother."

"Katherine," Mom said in her harshest voice. "The Wilders are coming to dinner and if you wish to dine with us, I insist you dress for dinner and use your manners."

Kate leaned back, draping her arm over the back of the chair. "I'm not six years old anymore, Mommy. You don't scare me."

I needed to take lessons from my sister.

"It's called common decency, Katherine."

Kate took a sip from her glass and seemed to think about Mom's statement for a moment, and then she pursed her lips. "We could talk about common decency—" she turned her gaze to our mother, "—but considering that it's

Christmas Day and you want to keep everything civil, I'll save it for another time." She lifted her glass in salute. "See? I *can* behave."

It was going to be an interesting day.

Chapter Two
Joe

Christmas dinner was more than slightly uncomfortable. The Wilders showed up a few minutes after noon in their Sunday finest. They took one look at my sister, still dressed in her grunge outfit, and I could tell they were reconsidering their plans for the afternoon, but my mother rushed out of her seat faster than I'd seen her move in ages and grabbed Hilary's mother's arm, probably to keep her from bolting.

"Vanessa and Ed, we're so happy you're here. And thank you for loaning your lovely Hilary to us last night. I think it's good to start the tradition of our grandchild being here on Christmas morning."

"Like the baby knows," Kate laughed. "It's a cluster of cells."

"Katherine." Based on the look of surprise on Mom's face, the one-word admonishment had come out sounding harsher than she'd intended. But then Kate had always been good at pushing Mom's buttons.

"Mother." Kate lifted her eyebrows and smirked, daring our mother to continue.

Flustered, Mom announced it was time for dinner, and we all headed into the massive dining room and sat at the mahogany table. I'd had more elaborate, multi-course meals at that table than I could count, but it had become a talisman that evoked only one memory—the disastrous dinner Rose and I had attended here only a few short months ago. The anger over that night had burned in my gut for so long, it was still smoldering embers. It only needed a little poking to rear its ugly head. I'd spent several weeks trying to come to terms with Rose's decision to be with Mason. But that damned table was just another kick in the gut.

Kate stopped behind me, standing on her tiptoes so that her mouth barely reached my shoulder. She whispered, "You and I need to chat later."

I glanced down at her in surprise. When she left two years ago, she'd made it clear that she was through with me and the entire Simmons mess. I couldn't help but wonder what she'd heard—and from whom—to incite her return. I planned to find out.

My parents sat on either end of the table, with me and Hilary on one side and Kate and the Wilders on the other. Kate sat directly in front of me, and both of us were positioned at the end of the table next to our father. No doubt the seating had been planned strategically, as my mother was unable to control herself around my unconventional sister.

The conversation was stilted during the first two courses, while everyone waited for the ticking time bomb that sat across from me to explode. But Kate surprisingly kept most of her snide comments to herself.

Everyone ignored her for the most part, but I finally asked her the question I'd been dying to have answered. "Kate, where've you been for the last two years?"

Mom glanced at Hilary's parents, then shot me a glare. "Joe, I'm sure the Wilders don't want to hear about Katherine's exploits."

I grinned at my sister. "Oh, I'm not so sure about that. They'll probably be entertained."

"I could go into all the drugs and booze and men…" She rolled her eyes dramatically. "Oh, the men."

I laughed. How could I have forgotten her sense of humor and flair for drama? It was entertaining as long as it wasn't directed at me.

Hilary cringed, her hand tightening around her butter knife enough to slightly lift it off the table.

I cast her a curious glance. Was Hilary capable of violence? She'd been in the Arkansas State Police with me, but her position had mostly been a desk job. Though she'd carried a gun, it had never been used in the line of duty. Still, the looks she was shooting my sister made me wonder.

"Maybe you should leave out those particular exploits," I said with a wink.

"Then that hardly leaves me anything to tell." Kate held up her wine glass, swirling the liquid before inhaling the scent and taking a sip. Her outward appearance was a sharp contrast to her actions now. In fact, it was a sharp contrast to her upbringing. The art of acting proper while attending a dinner party had been pounded into us before we even started middle school. Kate had been raised in this world with me, but she'd thrown off the mantle and blazed her own trail. Looking at her now, I couldn't tell if she was happy or not, but I was dying to know. I had to know if it was possible for me too.

If Mason Deveraux succeeded in his fanatical quest to bring down my father, I would have the chance to truly be free. But like a man who was faced with the prospect of freedom after spending his life in prison, I found myself unsure of what I really wanted. Had Kate figured that puzzle out for herself?

When we were served pie and coffee, Kate decided it was time to turn her attention to the woman beside me.

"So, Hils. Whatcha up to these days?"

Hilary's fork continued its sideways slice through the pecan pie on her plate. She scooped the bite onto the tines, then glanced at my sister. "I've taken a leave of absence from the state police."

"Because you're pregnant?" Kate's voice was deceptively vacant of emotion.

"Yes." Hilary lifted her fork to her mouth, her hand tightly gripping the handle.

Kate leaned her elbows on the table, tilting closer to Hilary. "I'm not sure if you've heard or not, but it's the twenty-first century. Pregnant woman are allowed to go out in public and have jobs up until the time they deliver."

"Katherine," our mother interrupted. "Hilary worked for the state *police*. She couldn't very well put the next Simmons heir in danger."

Kate sat back in her chair, shaking her head in disgust. "There are so many things wrong with that statement. For one thing, Hilary basically had a desk job."

But how did Kate know that? Hilary had only started her new position with the state police a few months before my sister took off.

Hilary set her fork down and lifted her finely waxed eyebrows. "I was at a big bust in Henryetta last June. We took down a criminal mastermind."

"The way I heard it, you only became involved because you found out Joe had met someone." She turned and looked at me. "Is that true, Joe? Did you meet someone in Henryetta, Arkansas?"

How did Kate know so much about our lives, particularly since we knew next to nothing about hers? But that question ranked lower on my priority list than my resolve never to discuss Rose at this table again. I gave my sister a menacing glare. "Not now, Kate," I said through gritted teeth.

She appraised me for a second before glancing away, seeming to recognize she'd pushed too far. It was like she was sending out feelers, seeing what was and wasn't acceptable to me, although she didn't seem to care about establishing that boundary with anyone else.

Turning away from me, Kate returned her attention to Hilary, a wicked gleam in her eyes. "What exactly have you done in Henryetta besides screw up the report of what happened in the Crocker bust?"

Screw up the report? And how did she know about Daniel Crocker, and why? I shifted in my seat. "What are you talking about?"

But Kate ignored me as the two women embarked on a staring contest. "Hilary knows exactly what I'm talking about. We both know why she was in Henryetta in June and what her real purpose was."

Mom's face reddened. "Katherine, I won't allow you to destroy Christmas dinner for our guests."

Vanessa looked down at her plate, but irritation crept over Ed's face. Surprisingly, my father merely observed it all.

"Guests." Kate laughed. "Please. Besides, you have to admit things have been drop-dead boring since I left." She took a sip of her wine, keeping her gaze on Hilary. "But you still didn't answer my original question. What are you up to these days besides incubating the Simmons heir?"

Hilary lifted her chin. "I was helping Joe with his campaign for state senate."

"Yeah, I heard that didn't go so well. Except for your little souvenir." Kate uncurled her index finger from her wine glass and pointed at Hilary's stomach. "But that was almost two months ago. What are you doing *now?*"

Hilary's cheeks went pink. "I'm living in Henryetta."

"With Joe?"

Hilary's forehead wrinkled. "No."

Kate chuckled, then said in wonderment, "Hilary Wilder living in Henryetta, Arkansas. Is this some type of community service project?"

"Katherine," Mom said with more force. "That is enough."

Kate kept any more questions to herself, but we both knew her goal had been achieved. My sister may have been gone two years, but it had taken her hardly any time at all to pick up her favorite pastime: tormenting Hilary.

Mom cleared her throat. "Why don't we adjourn to the living room to exchange gifts?"

She ushered us back into the living room so she could pass out presents. It was a ridiculous waste of time and money. We gave each other the same gifts every year. I made a charitable contribution in my parents' name to the American Heart Association in honor of my grandfather. My parents gave me several dress shirts. Then there were several insignificant yet expensive gifts for the Wilders, Hilary included. While there weren't any gifts for Kate—which she found amusing—there were a slew of presents for Hilary's baby.

Hilary's baby.

It was funny how much trouble I had acknowledging it was mine. I hoped I could somehow find it in me to love him or her despite the way I felt about the mother. But I figured I still had seven or so months to sort out my feelings.

Hilary opened boxes of expensive baby clothes, knit blankets, and even a silver rattle. As soon as she opened the last present, I decided I'd fulfilled my responsibility. I looked at my phone and stood. "Well, this has been fun as always, but I need to get back to Fenton County for my shift. Kate, could you walk me out?"

"Leave? That's ridiculous," my mother said, a scowl deepening the crow's feet around her eyes. "It's Christmas, Joe. You should use your elevated position to your advantage."

I gave her a wry smile. "While that seems to be the Simmons way, I've decided to take a different tactic."

Kate studied me as though she was trying to figure me out, but I didn't have time to say anything to her because Dad said, "Hold on, Joe. I need to talk to you before you go." He stood. "In the office."

My heart thudded against my ribcage. Why would he want to talk to me alone? This couldn't be good news, and

I was terrified it either had something to do with Rose or—worse and much more likely—Mason's continued pursuit for incriminating evidence against my father.

Hilary looked up at me with a pretty pout. "I was hoping we could drive back to Henryetta together."

I shook my head and gave her a glare that let her know I thought she was crazy. "But we drove up in separate cars. How would you get yours back to Henryetta?"

She sighed. "Well, will you at least take some of the baby's gifts back with you? I'm not sure they'll all fit in my car."

I wasn't sure why she wanted to take them back at all. Our parents were sure to coerce her to move back to El Dorado when her plans to strong-arm me into marrying her fell through. But if agreeing got me out of my parents' house faster, I'd do it, even if it meant I'd have to see her sooner than I'd like in Henryetta. "Fine. But have Gerald put them in my car now. As soon as I'm done talking to Dad, I'm out of here."

Dad headed to the office and I followed on his heels. The familiar arrangement put me in mind of dozens of memories, none of them pleasant. When I was a kid, the walk to my father's office—always behind him—had always filled me with terror, and this time wasn't any different. The stakes were so much higher than they'd ever been.

He walked through the threshold and—without looking back—said, "Shut the door behind you." His instruction was unnecessary and we both knew it, just as we both knew he was saying it to let me know I was on his turf and he was in total control.

He moved behind his desk and sat in the creaky leather chair. "Take a seat, Joe. We have a few things to discuss."

I sat in one of the chairs in front of his desk, trying to keep my gaze from the whiskey decanter on the table against the wall. If ever I needed a drink, it was now, but I put both hands on the chair's arms and stared at him with a look of studied indifference.

He waited for several seconds in an effort to make me squirm, but I managed to wait him out without reacting.

"Do you know where Mason Deveraux was last week?" he finally asked.

I blinked in surprise. That was probably the last question I expected. "Do I look like Mason Deveraux's keeper?"

"That's not an answer."

I shrugged away my confusion. "How should I know? He doesn't clear his schedule with me."

"You're telling me that the chief deputy sheriff didn't know the ADA was out of pocket for three days?"

How close of tabs did he keep on Deveraux? "I knew he took several days off, but he'd just been in a car accident. Not to mention the fact that he nearly died in a fire the night of that big strip club bust. I didn't think anything of it."

"He was in Little Rock."

I tried to hide my surprise. "So? His mother just sold her home there and moved to Henryetta. Maybe he was in town to tie up the loose ends."

"He was in the offices of the state capitol."

"Why don't you stop beating around the bush and tell me what you think you know, since I obviously don't know anything."

"I think he was there snooping on me."

I took a slow steady breath, trying to hide my sudden anxiety. Was my father right? It wouldn't surprise me if that's exactly what Deveraux had been doing, and if so, it had been smart of him not to tell me. "I think you're paranoid. Why would he be snooping on you?"

"He's dating your old girlfriend. Does she know about the information I have on her?"

That question caught me by surprise, although I wasn't sure why. To tell him yes would put Deveraux in a dangerous place, but would my father really buy that I hadn't told Rose anything? In the end, it was a moot point; my hesitation was all he needed to confirm his hunch.

"Of course she'd tell her ADA boyfriend. The question is what he's planning to do about it."

"You don't know that. She was embarrassed by it."

He raised an eyebrow. "Are you really going to sit there and tell me that she wouldn't confide in the one man who would help her?"

The one man who would help her. That statement stung more than he'd probably intended, but he was right. When I found out that my father had fabricated evidence suggesting Rose hired Daniel Crocker to murder her mother, I'd toed the line and run for office. My course of action after discovering the trap my father had set for Rose—a trap he could set off at any moment—was to wait him out. But Mason wasn't that kind of man. My father knew it and so did Rose. Still, I'd warned Deveraux how dangerous his path was, and he'd rushed headlong down it anyway.

Dammit.

"Mason Deveraux is not a stupid man," I said. "He knows how dangerous it would be to tangle with you. I'm sure he was in Little Rock on Fenton County business. He was just part of a sting operation for the county. Perhaps he was in Little Rock working on that."

"Deveraux needs to let sleeping dogs lie."

My eyes narrowed. "What does that mean?"

He paused, then smiled. "How's your new position in the sheriff's office working out?"

My father never did anything without a purpose. So why was he asking about my job after mentioning Mason's involvement in the sting operation? "It's going great."

"You have the potential to make a name for yourself there."

I couldn't help but wonder where this was going. "I seem to be settling in."

"That failed bust on Thanksgiving was a mark against you, but the one last week will definitely be an asset."

I wasn't surprised he was keeping a score sheet.

"The Fenton County sheriff is going to announce his retirement and you will run for his position."

My eyes widened. "You want me to stay in Fenton County? Mom wants me to move back to El Dorado."

His lips pressed together, showing his displeasure. "We all know who will win this disagreement."

While it stuck in my craw that my father was dictating yet another career move for me, the idea of running for sheriff actually felt right.

"But there's still too much turmoil in Fenton County. It needs to die down, or your race won't be the shoo-in it should be." He paused and placed both palms on his desk. "I want you to take care of the organized crime problem in town."

I shifted in my seat. "What do you think those last two big busts have been about?"

"The new crime lord needs to disappear."

I gaped at him. "Skeeter Malcolm?" While it didn't surprise me to hear that my father had been keeping tabs on the situation in Henryetta, I hadn't expected him to show this much interest in the nitty-gritty details.

"You need to listen carefully." He paused to make sure he had my attention. "There are pieces in play that you don't need to know about. In fact, considering your position, it's best for you to stay in the dark. But it's in everyone's best interest for Mr. Malcolm to lose his crown."

My mind raced to connect the dots. "My job is to deal with the criminal elements in Henryetta. While it might look as though I've been unsuccessful, we were very close to apprehending the owner of the strip club last week. He's become a major player in the crime world in my area. We have leads on where he might be holed up."

"Back off on his apprehension."

I hesitated, trying to let his message sink in. Since when did my father concern himself with Fenton County matters? It was two counties away, and he'd always considered it a cesspool. "Why would I do that?"

"He has his role to play, and so do you."

I shook my head in disbelief. "You want me to let an alleged murderer escape?"

"I expect you to do as I say."

"I'm not five years old, and this is much bigger than J.R. Simmons getting his way. This man is armed and dangerous. The citizens in my county won't be safe until he's apprehended."

"If Malcolm disappears, things will die down."

What exactly was my father proposing? "So essentially you're telling me to let a murderer and thief get off scot-free so he can murder a man and become the next crime lord."

"While it sounds base, it's important to look at the bigger picture, Joe."

Base. So he really wanted me to do it. He wanted me to allow this underworld criminal to kill Malcolm, then take over for him. But my previous undercover work served me well. I hid any sign of surprise, acting intrigued instead. "Which is?"

He sat back in his chair. "Your job is to make the county feel safe."

"No," I said, trying to keep my voice calm and even. "My job is to actually *keep* the citizens safe, not fabricate the illusion of safety."

"You will do as I say in this, Joseph."

"I need a reason."

"No, the only thing you need to know is that I want this matter left alone."

"So I'm supposed to tell my deputies to back off and let Mick Gentry get away. And then I just wait for him to take care of Malcolm?"

"It's as simple as that."

None of this made sense, not that I was actually planning to go through with it. Why would J.R. Simmons care about Skeeter Malcolm and Mick Gentry? The real question was what was in it for him? But if he had developed an interest in the crime world, perhaps Rose had been correct about suspecting his involvement in another matter. "What do you know about Deveraux's car accident? Did you know it wasn't an accident?"

His eyebrows rose. "Why would I care if he lives or dies?"

"Don't pretend you didn't just suggest he's meddling in your affairs."

He chuckled. "That hardly seems worthy of murder."

"So you're saying you don't know anything about it?"

He gave a half shrug. "There's a reason Mason Deveraux is in Fenton County. The previous ADA was a little too nosy. When Deveraux left Little Rock, he was apathetic. He was the perfect man for the job." He paused. "Some citizens expected him to continue that trend."

"So his sudden interest in justice for the citizens of Fenton County, combined with your paranoid delusions that he's interested in your dirt, made you put a hit on him?"

His head jutted back in surprise. "You think I put a hit on the ADA in Fenton County?" He began to laugh. "Your imagination has run wild, boy."

He'd pulled out the *boy*. I'd hit a nerve. "I will not condone the murder of Mason Deveraux."

His lips twitched with a barely repressed grin. "Your life would be easier without him."

I had to admit there was some truth to his statement. "So you're suggesting I sit back and let him be murdered too?"

He laughed again. "Do you really think I would dirty my hands by having a hit placed on someone? It's not my style."

"But you know someone who wants him dead, don't you?"

He took a deep breath and blew it out. "Considering the short period of time he held his position in Little Rock, he prosecuted an amazing number of very powerful and very disgruntled men. Any number of whom wouldn't bat an eye at seeking retribution."

So a criminal was after Deveraux. Rose wasn't safe. But I needed more answers, which meant keeping my cool. "What gives me the idea that you know which disgruntled criminal is behind it?"

He grinned, his eyes twinkling. "You give me far too much credit. I'm just an observer in this situation."

None of this made sense, but there was no denying he had me freaked out. "I can't sit back and let this happen."

"But if you don't know any details, how can you put a stop to it?" He leaned his elbow on the arm of his chair. "Which brings me to another topic." His brow furrowed. "You will propose to Hilary and marry her within the next few months."

"You can't be serious."

"Totally."

"I don't love her. I don't even *like* her."

"You *liked* her enough to get her pregnant."

I stifled a cringe. "I'm not going to live in a loveless marriage."

"Consider it a marriage of convenience. It won't be the first and it won't be the last. Besides," he said with a smirk. "Look how your last love-based relationship worked out."

I clenched my fists. "You are unbelievable," I spat out in disgust. "Our breakup had nothing to with our feelings for each other. You were going to make her give up her entire life for me."

He looked unimpressed. "She claimed she loved you, but she wouldn't sacrifice for you. You were willing to give up your entire life for *her*."

"That was different!" I rose to my feet and shouted. "I actually wanted that life. I still do. Why do you think I moved there?"

He pressed his back into his seat, then placed his hands together in front of him, as if puzzling out a particularly perplexing riddle. "You still want that girl. Even now."

"You know her name. At least do me the respect of saying it."

My father studied the wall for several seconds before turning to look at me with a gleam of excitement in his eyes. "What if I told you I would give you my blessing to marry Rose Gardner?"

I shook my head. "She won't marry me. She already refused your conditions."

He held his hands out, palms up. "No conditions."

My mouth dropped open. "You're saying I can marry her without her changing anything in her life? She can keep all of her friends and continue working at the nursery?"

"I said no conditions."

I shook my head, but my heart beat fast with excitement. "I don't get it. Five seconds ago you ordered me to marry Hilary."

"I realize now that I might have been wrong about the situation."

My father rarely admitted to mistakes, but this was no time to gloat. "There's obviously something in it for you."

"I'll let you marry Rose Gardner, but only if you do as I ask in regards to the Fenton County situation."

There had to be something huge brewing in Fenton County if my father was willing to allow Hilary to give birth to a Simmons bastard in exchange for my cooperation. "I let Gentry murder Skeeter Malcolm?"

"He's a criminal, Joe. Malcolm got himself into this situation. You're just allowing the natural order of things to take place."

"And Mason Deveraux?"

"Call it a blessing in disguise."

Chapter Three

Rose

Every Christmas before this one had been a mixed blessing. While I loved spending time with my Aunt Bessie and Uncle Earl, Momma had always gone out of her way to make the day difficult for me. After learning some of the details about Daddy's affair with my birth mother, Dora, I finally understood why she'd treated me poorly, and with Jonah's help, I was working on forgiving her.

But Christmas this year was everything I'd always hoped it would be. We gathered together at the farmhouse my birth mother had owned—me, Mason, his mother, Violet and the kids, Jonah, and Bruce Wayne. The only ones missing were Mike—who was spending the day with his parents—Aunt Bessie and Uncle Earl, who'd gone on a cruise with their friends, and Neely Kate, who was with her crazy family. She'd texted to tell me that Ronnie had begun drinking around ten in the morning in preparation for a day with her cousins.

When we sat down to Christmas dinner, I looked around the table, thankful to be blessed with so much love and friendship.

But if I were honest, part of me wondered how Joe was doing. Christmas had been difficult for both of us growing up, so when we were together we'd promised each other to make this Christmas a holiday neither one of us would ever forget. Now I was surprised that I found myself wondering if he was spending the day with his parents. It made me sad to think of him being sent back to the prison of his past when I'd escaped mine. But I reminded myself that I wasn't responsible for Joe's happiness. While I knew that to be true, why did it weigh so heavy on my heart anyway?

I glanced up at Mason and my chest warmed when I found him looking at me with unabashed love. I reached my hand toward him and he took it in his and squeezed.

"How was your trip?" Violet asked, scooping a small helping of lasagna onto Mikey's plate. Violet hadn't been happy that I'd decided to go non-traditional with the meal, but she hadn't put up too much of a fuss either. It was more progress for us.

I blinked at her in surprise. "What trip?"

She looked up and scowled. "I know you left town for a few days, Rose Gardner, so don't you try to lie to me."

Crappy doodles.

I glanced at Mason, unsure of what to say. He'd taken a short trip to Little Rock, and he'd given me the early Christmas gift of a girls' trip to New Orleans with Neely Kate to see the musical *Wicked.* But he'd asked me not to tell anyone, not even Violet. And although he'd refused to tell me why, I suspected it had more to do with his trip to Little Rock than it did with my vacation with Neely Kate. Still, I'd respected his wishes, so I had no idea how my sister had figured it out.

"Maeve stopped by the nursery and she had Muffy with her."

Mason's mother gave me an apologetic look. "I'm sorry. I didn't realize it was a secret."

Mason squeezed my hand, then cleared his throat. "It wasn't necessarily a secret. It all just came together quickly."

Violet pinned my boyfriend with her gaze. "Where did you go?"

"Rose and Neely Kate were in New Orleans while I was in Little Rock on business."

Violet's mouth dropped. "You went to New Orleans? *Alone?*"

"I wasn't alone. I had Neely Kate with me." My shoulders tensed as I waited for her verbal berating.

"That's amazing, Rose. You've never been so far from Henryetta! Did you have fun?"

I let out a sigh of relief that she wasn't holding this over my head. "It was an interesting experience." If you called being a murder suspect, and Neely Kate seeing a ghost *interesting.*

Mason picked up the bread basket and winked at me. "Rose and Neely Kate seem to find excitement wherever they go."

Violet shook her head. "No kidding. I can't believe you were at…*that place* last week," she finished, substituting *that place* for *strip club*. "Do you know how dangerous that was?"

I glanced at Ashley, my five-year-old niece, who was intently watching our conversation. "Violet." I widened my eyes. "I think you're exaggerating." I shot my gaze back to Ashley to send her a silent message.

Violet's lips pressed together. "We'll discuss this more tomorrow at the shop when we finalize the plans for the grand reopening."

"Okay." We were in the home stretch for reopening the nursery and launching my landscaping business. We'd only just opened the nursery a few months ago, and although vandalism of the store had forced us to close for the entire Christmas season, I saw no reason for reopening with any pomp and circumstance. Given the way Henryetta was still gossiping about my sister's affair with Mayor Brody MacIntosh, I'd prefer to keep it quiet.

We spent the rest of dinner hearing about the kids' Christmas gifts, Bruce Wayne's first Christmas Eve with his biological father's family, and Jonah's stint on Jeopardy.

"It was a nerve-racking experience," Jonah said, wearing an ear-to-ear grin. "But I think my experience on camera helped with my nerves."

"So how'd you do?" Mason asked.

Jonah's grin turned ornery. "You'll just have to wait and see when it airs." He picked up his glass of water. "I'm bound to secrecy until then."

"Not even a hint?" Violet asked, and when Jonah pressed his lips together to prove his point, she said, "Then tell us about your new girlfriend."

Jonah's cheeks turned rosy. "I'm not sure what there is to tell."

I smiled at my friend. His relationship with Jessica was still so new, but I could tell he was happy. He'd even taken her with him to California for the taping of his Jeopardy episode the previous week.

"She's the church secretary," I volunteered. "And she's had a crush on him since he hired her."

Jonah's blush deepened. "I wouldn't be with her at all if Rose hadn't intervened."

"I'd like to think you would have found the courage to ask her out."

Once Jonah got over his uncharacteristic bashfulness, he told us a bit about Jessica. She'd been born and raised outside of Henryetta, and she came from a large family. "Three brothers and five sisters."

"Wow," Mason said, taking another helping of garlic bread. "That's a lot of kids."

"She says she only wants a couple of her own."

Jonah and Jessica were getting serious quick if they were already discussing children.

But while Jonah seemed totally at ease, I noticed that Bruce Wayne was quiet and more withdrawn than usual. He was typically a shy man, but I suspected something else was going on with him. I planned to corner him the next day to find out.

Everyone stayed well into the evening, laughing and having a good time. After our guests left, I stood in the kitchen doorway, looking at the last bit of mess left over from dessert. Mason walked up behind me and pressed his stomach against my back, wrapping his arms around my front.

"I'll help you clean it up tomorrow night."

I glanced up at him in surprise. With the long hours he worked, he always made sure to eat breakfast with me and clean up the kitchen before he left.

He grimaced. "I have to leave early tomorrow."

He'd checked his cell phone several times during dinner, but he'd put it in his pocket when he noticed me watching. What was going on? Now I was really curious. "I thought you had a light week since it's between Christmas and New Year's."

"I was off for several days, so I need to catch up."

I spun around in his arms and looked up into his face. "What were you doing in Little Rock?"

"Official Fenton County business, Ms. Gardner."

That was my cue to butt out. Too bad for Mason I didn't back down so easily. "Why did you want me out of town while you were gone?"

He grinned. "I was under the mistaken impression you'd be safer out of town."

I gave him an indignant glare. "What happened in New Orleans wasn't my fault, Mason. I couldn't help that the psychic Neely Kate went to see was murdered after Neely Kate threatened her."

"I never said it was your fault. But I've pretty much decided that I should plan on trouble finding you wherever you go, and with that knowledge in mind, it was probably a mistake to send you to New Orleans of all places."

I wrapped my hands around his neck. "Then where would you rather send me?"

His lips lowered to mine. "Our bed. You're more than welcome to cause all the trouble you want there."

He was clearly distracting me, but I knew when to pick my battles. I'd find out tomorrow. He had his sinfully evil ways and so did I.

***

The next morning, Mason's alarm woke me and I was surprised to see it was still dark outside. He turned it off and pulled me to his side, nuzzling the top of my head.

"Why are you getting up so early?" I murmured.

"I already told you." But he pulled me closer.

I propped up on my elbow and searched his face, barely able to make out his features in the dark. "No, you didn't. Instead of answering my question, you distracted me."

He grinned lazily. "I didn't hear any arguments."

"Mason, I'm serious. I understand you can't tell me certain things about your work, but you need to tell me if it's important. I had a right to know about your sting operation last week."

His grin faded. "Rose, I couldn't tell you."

"Why?" I asked, getting indignant. "Did you really think I was going to blow your cover?"

"No." He sat up. "Of course not."

I sat up with him and turned to face him. "Then why did you keep it a secret?"

He took my hand and searched my face. "Sweetheart, it's not that I don't trust you. I would trust you with my life. But you know that, officially, I *can't* tell you."

"That's not fair, Mason."

He was silent and looked out the window, as if searching for an answer out there.

"You could have been killed—no, you *would* have been killed—if I hadn't been there."

"Rose," he said, sounding more gruff. "If you hadn't been there, things might have turned out differently."

"What does that mean?" I asked, getting angry. "Are you insinuating that I messed up whatever it was you were doin'? Because the way I remember it, you were about to be tossed out on your behind when I showed up."

He rubbed his forehead. "I still might have been able to salvage the situation."

My mouth dropped open. "You *do* think I messed it up!"

"I didn't say that."

"You didn't have to." I slid out of bed and padded to the bathroom, flipping on the light.

Mason followed me and stood in the doorway. "Rose, look, I understand why you felt it was necessary to go to Gems that night."

I grabbed my toothbrush and looked at his reflection in the mirror. "*Do you?* You think I was there looking for Dolly Parton, right? Well, there was a lot more to it."

He had the good sense to keep quiet, his eyes focused on mine in the mirror.

"A good part of the reason I was there was to save *you*, Mason Van de Camp Deveraux. I thought you might be caught in something that would get you in trouble, and I was there to help you get out of it."

He was silent for a moment, his body rigid. "I still can't believe that you thought I was taking bribes. You really think I'd commit the crime I'm trying to fight."

"I didn't say that," I said, repeating his words from a few moments before.

His eyes turned cold. "You didn't have to," he said, throwing my words back at me. He turned around and left the bathroom.

I ditched the toothbrush and followed him. "I didn't think the worst of you, Mason."

He pulled open a drawer and rummaged for a pair of underwear and socks. "So there's a *good side* to someone taking bribes?"

I grabbed his arm and made him look at me. "I thought you might have been blackmailed. I couldn't imagine that you would do something like that unless your hand had been forced…or if you were offered something you needed."

"Money?" he asked, making the word sound dirty.

Tears burned my eyes. "No. Something to help save me from J.R. Simmons."

His anger faded and he closed his eyes. "God, Rose. I'm sorry."

I wrapped my arms around his back and pressed my cheek to his chest. "No, don't say you're sorry. Sometimes I wish I'd never told you about J.R. Simmons' threats."

His arms stiffened. "You'd rather keep it a secret from me?"

"I'd rather keep you *safe*. Now you're putting yourself in danger on this quest to stop him and I'm terrified for you." My voice broke. "I can't lose you, Mason. Especially not like this."

His arms tightened around me. "I only want to protect you. Can't you understand that?"

"I understand it only too well. But you're going to get hurt."

"Not if I'm careful."

I leaned back and looked into his face. "Mason, you have to tell me exactly what it is you're doin'. The not knowing is making my imagination run wild and it's scaring the bejiggers out of me. Someone tried to kill you last week. How can you be so sure J.R. Simmons wasn't behind it?"

Skeeter Malcolm thought his own turncoat men were the perpetrators, but I wasn't convinced. Occasional visions were my only precognition "gift," but some deep instinct told me I was right. There was more to this story than met the eye.

Mason cupped my cheek in his hand and looked into my eyes. "Sweetheart, it was Mick Gentry and his men."

"He said it wasn't."

"He's a murderer and a liar. His word doesn't mean much."

This was getting me nowhere in my quest to make him stop, so I took another tactic. "I know your trip to Little Rock had something to do with J.R. Simmons. Admit it."

Though he didn't look away, his jaw tightened slightly. "I was there on off-the-record business."

"J.R. Simmons business."

"I can't tell you everything, Rose."

"You're not telling me *anything*."

"It's safer for you that way."

"*Why?* He already wants to hurt me. It's not like he'll be any more or less inclined to go after me if you tell me what you're doing."

He released a heavy sigh. "It's not necessarily J.R. Simmons I'm worried about. You could be considered an accomplice."

It took several seconds for his words to sink in. "You're doing something illegal to help me," I whispered.

"I love you, Rose. I *will* protect you." He stared into my eyes as he said it, his gaze filled with fierce resolution.

I shook my head. "*No.* We'll find another way."

"I have to get ready. We'll talk about this more tonight." He kissed me gently and stooped to pull out more clothes from a drawer.

"Where are you going?" I asked as he shut the drawer.

"Sweetheart, I promise you this is official business."

"About J.R. Simmons?"

"No." He groaned. "Rose, you have to trust me." He stood in the doorway to the bathroom and watched me. "Do you trust me?"

Trust was a two-way street. Mason had a chest full of secrets that he kept locked away in the name of Fenton County business and my own safety, and while that irked me to no end, I couldn't deny I had plenty of secrets of my own. Huge ones that could potentially destroy his career if they ever came to light. But one thing I knew without a doubt about this man was that he loved me and was determined to keep me safe. And at the moment, that scared me more than all the half-truths and lies of omission. "It's not that simple, Mason. There are many ways to trust or distrust someone."

I expected him to get angry, but he gave a short nod instead. "Okay, fair enough. Do you trust that I'm telling you the truth about my meeting?"

I studied his face. "Yes."

"Then that's a good start."

A good start. As he turned to go into the bathroom, I couldn't help wondering how we'd jumped back to the beginning.

Chapter Four
Joe

Winter in southern Arkansas is a fickle bitch. One minute she's warm and sunny and you only have to wear a light coat, then the next day she'll throw freezing rain at you.

Today, she was in fine form.

It matched my mood.

I almost called Deveraux to cancel our meeting. The county road crew had taken care of the highways, but they hadn't gotten out to the county roads yet, and while the roads weren't completely iced over, they had enough slick patches to make driving treacherous. Of course, it might not have been so bad if we'd met at the courthouse or somewhere in town, but after my chat with my father the previous day, I figured that other than official sanctioned Fenton County business, the less we were seen together in public, the better. For both of us.

Which was why I suggested we meet somewhere out of the ordinary. And now it was biting me in the ass as my car slipped and slid on the unsalted paved road.

I'd driven past the deserted gas station on County Road 110 over a dozen times, including on my drive home from El Dorado the previous afternoon. It had occurred to me that it would be great hidden meeting spot. The nearby woods had reclaimed part of the gravel parking lot on the right side, and the left was angled back enough that someone could park a car behind it without being noticed from the road. But Deveraux had only been in Fenton County for seven months, and he'd spent most of his time at the courthouse. When I suggested that we meet at the Sinclair station, he couldn't place where it was until I mentioned the giant faded dinosaur in front.

His car was idling behind the building, but I didn't notice it until I pulled around the corner. It really was the perfect location for clandestine meetings, and though I appreciated that fact for my present purposes, I filed away a reminder to myself to check the place more often for mischievous activities.

Deveraux got out of his car as soon as I pulled up, and the scowl on his face let me know he wasn't in a good mood. I unlocked the door so he could slide into the passenger seat.

I didn't waste any time. "What were you doing in Little Rock last week?"

If he was surprised by my question, he didn't let on. "I'm not sure why you care, *Chief Deputy*."

"Cut the shit, Deveraux. My father knows."

His jaw tightened and he looked out the windshield into the trees. "And…?"

"And he wants to know why you were there."

"What did you tell him?"

"That I didn't have a freaking clue."

He turned to face me, but his eyes were guarded. "And he bought it?"

"Yeah, because it was true."

He turned back to face the windshield. "And that's exactly why I'm not going to tell you."

"He's watching you like a hawk, Deveraux."

"I'm not surprised."

"Did it ever occur to you that you're putting Rose in *more* danger?"

He didn't answer. I considered telling Deveraux that I had a way of saving Rose from my father's blackmail—one that would allow him to back out of his crazy scheme—but I knew he'd never go for it. Besides, I wanted to get more answers before I volunteered any information.

I had to know far he planned to go. "Did you take her with you?"

His jaw tightened. "Maybe you should ask Rose."

My temper flared. "I'm asking you, you asshole. The only reason I've put up with any of this is because I was deluded into thinking you could protect her, but from what I can see, you're just making things worse." I took a breath and forced myself to calm down before continuing. "Now where the hell was she? Because she sure as hell wasn't here." He started to say something, but I interrupted, "I know Muffy was at Maeve's."

This time he was the one to show surprise. Of course, he had no idea how much time I'd spent at his mother's house lately. He probably figured I knew about Muffy from Violet.

"She was in New Orleans with Neely Kate."

"New Orleans?" Something pinched in my heart, catching me by surprise. Rose had never left the state of Arkansas before, despite the fact that Henryetta was so close to the Louisiana border. Over the summer, I used to suggest that I could drive her over the state line just for the sake of it, but she'd always insist that when she left the state, it would be for a real purpose, not just to say she'd done it. I'd always thought I'd be the one to take her, although it made sense she would do it with someone else now. But the knowledge still hurt.

"I wanted her to be out of town while I was gone, and I asked her not to tell anyone she was leaving or where she was going."

"Why?"

"Because *I know* your father is watching. And because someone tried to kill me last week. What's to keep them from going after Rose next? I didn't want her with me in Little Rock, but I wasn't about to let her stay here by herself, either. I figured she'd be safe if she left town without telling anyone. How many more reasons would you like?"

My back stiffened. "You think she's not safe here? I would have watched out for her."

"She doesn't *want* you to watch out for her. She would have insisted on staying at the farm, and you know it." He turned and glared at me. "And before you can say it, *no* you would *not* have stayed there with her. Not after the way you accosted her in November."

I fought to regain control. "You're a rebound, Deveraux. She thinks she wants you, but she'll figure out the truth sooner rather than later."

He reached for the door handle. "Since we've resorted to this part of the conversation, are we done?"

I groaned. "No. That's not our only problem."

He sat back in the seat. "Go on."

"My father and I had a chat before I left yesterday, and like our conversation this morning, it started with the purpose of your visit to Little Rock. Then it moved on to another topic."

"Which was…?"

"The Fenton County crime world."

Deveraux turned completely to face me.

I continued, "He wants me to back off on arresting Mick Gentry."

His eyelid twitched. "Why?"

"He wants the criminal elements in town to sort themselves out."

"And what does that mean?"

"He wants Skeeter Malcolm eliminated."

"He wants you to arrest him?"

"No. He wants Gentry to take care of him for us."

"He wants him *murdered*?"

"Yeah."

"And what did you say?"

I grabbed the steering wheel in a tight grip. "What the hell does that mean?"

"It's your father. Don't you pretty much jump and ask how high?"

I narrowed my eyes. "Do you really think I take my position as the chief deputy so casually?"

"If we threw your father out of the equation, I would say you're a great deputy. Better than this county has seen in decades." He paused and looked momentarily pained by the admission. "But we both know he has you on a short leash…and the woman we both love is at the end on a choke hold. You'll do whatever he tells you to do."

"Would you rather I didn't?"

He scowled. "No, but I don't like the idea of J.R. Simmons dictating how the Fenton County sheriff's department does its job."

"How do you think I feel?" As soon as the words left my mouth, I realized I'd set him up.

Shockingly, he didn't take the bait. "Why does your father want Malcolm out of the way?"

"I don't know, but I don't like it."

"And he wants Mick Gentry to take over as the kingpin?" he asked, incredulous.

"Or at least do the dirty work of taking care of Malcolm."

"But why does he care what goes on here?"

"He says the sheriff is going to announce his retirement. My father wants me to run. I think he's trying to make himself look good."

"That still doesn't explain why he cares about who runs the Fenton County underworld. Does J.R. Simmons have business here?"

I sighed. "Not that I knew about, but he mentioned something about you that makes me think he does."

"Me?"

I'd laid awake half the night trying to figure out what to tell Deveraux. I knew I had to be careful in what I said—and didn't say. "He claims he moved you to Fenton County because you were apathetic, and he suggested some of the citizens here might not like your newfound hunger for justice."

"Like my encounter with the much-loved Daniel Crocker." Mason's jaw tightened. "Your father has some stake here in Fenton County. Some illegal activity that Malcolm is impeding. Do you have any idea what it could be?"

"How the hell would I know?"

"He's your father."

"Here's a news flash for you, Deveraux," I said, my temper rising. "I'm in law enforcement for a reason."

"So you can cover up your daddy's illegal activities?"

"Is that why you think I'm here?"

"You're obviously considering kowtowing to him."

"Get the hell out of my car!"

He grabbed the door handle and shoved the door open. "Gladly."

After I watched him climb into his car and drive away, I wondered why I'd let myself lose control. But more importantly, I realized that I'd never told him there was someone out there who still wanted him dead.

Chapter Five
Mason

I pulled into my parking spot in front of the courthouse, but instead of getting out, I gripped the steering wheel and berated myself for the millionth time in the last twenty minutes.

My temper had gotten the best of me. I reached for my phone to call Simmons, but I decided to give it another hour. I was still pissed and I couldn't afford to lose it like I had earlier.

Dammit.

It didn't help that I'd gone into the meeting in a bad mood after my disagreement with Rose. Both Rose and Joe were right, of course. I'd been in Little Rock digging for dirt on J.R. Simmons. And while I hadn't come back with any hard evidence, I had found two promising leads. One was a possible bribery scheme in Columbia County involving a construction company getting a county government job.

The second was trickier. It involved a possible extortion scheme, and in Fenton County, no less. The only problem was that it had happened twenty-five years ago. It was definitely past the statute of limitations and worthless to me in terms of toppling J.R. Still, something nagged at me not to let it fall off my radar. Rumor had it that the shady dealings had gone down in the summer and fall of the year Rose's birth mother had died…and the company involved was the very one that had employed Dora Middleton.

What if her birth mother had somehow been involved?

And while part of me knew I should tell Rose, I'd kept it from her—along with everything else I'd learned in Little Rock—when I came home. It wasn't intentional. As soon as she came home, I learned that she and Neely Kate had been suspects in the murder of a psychic in New Orleans. She'd waved it off as nothing, saying that she hadn't called me for help while I was in Little Rock because she knew I was working on something important, and besides, there was nothing I could have done.

And that was the part that freaked me out the most. She could have been arrested for murder and I would have been powerless to help her.

Then I took it one step further: if J.R. Simmons pulled the trigger on his fabricated evidence, he was sure to have me removed from my position, and I'd be powerless in Fenton County too.

Finding solid evidence was the key to bringing Joe's father down, but I could have a stack of evidence against him and it wouldn't do me one iota of good if no one was willing to do anything with it. And one thing was certain—J.R. Simmons' reach was very deep in Arkansas.

It hadn't surprised me to learn he knew about my trip to Little Rock, but it meant he was watching me more closely than I'd suspected. Simmons hadn't gotten where he was by being stupid. He had to guess that Rose had told me about his fabricated evidence…and that I wouldn't sit by idly without trying to do something about it. Which meant I had to be even more careful.

I was still under the philosophy that the less Rose knew about my quest, the safer she'd be, but I realized that if I continued to keep things from her, I would risk losing her. Of course, I couldn't tell her everything about my work—the particulars of the sting operation Joe and I had been working on for the last few weeks had to be kept strictly confidential. And Joe had only agreed to help me dig up dirt on J.R. in a limited capacity so long as Rose didn't know about his involvement. But she had a right to know what I had discovered about J.R. Simmons. I just needed to be prepared to ignore her pleas for me to stop investigating.

I pulled up her name on my phone and called her, thankful when she answered. "Rose, I'm so sorry. Will you forgive me?"

She was silent for a moment and fear rooted in my gut. What if I'd pushed her too far? I was relieved when she finally said, "Of course, Mason. I know you think you're protecting me—"

"You're right, sweetheart, that's always been my reasoning, but I've realized it's wrong to keep you in the dark."

"You *have?*"

"I'm still not convinced it's the right thing to do, but you have the right to know."

"Thank you."

"But I still can't tell you everything," I warned. "I've promised some people I won't tell anyone they're involved."

"Okay. I understand."

"Can you meet me at Merilee's for lunch? Say noon."

"Of course."

"I love you, Rose. I hate when you're upset with me."

"I love you too, Mason. Everything's going to be okay."

I hoped she was right, not only about us, but about everything else too.

I hung up and stared at the courthouse. While I was sure Joe was keeping something things from me, I was fairly certain he'd told me the truth about everything else. The intention of my visit to Little Rock had been to find evidence incriminating J.R., but it looked like the proof I wanted was literally buried in my own backyard.

I pulled the keys out of my ignition and unlocked my glove compartment, then pulled out a burner phone I'd bought in Little Rock. If J.R. was watching me, I needed to be more careful with my calls. I stuck the phone in my coat pocket and headed up to the office.

My secretary looked up from her computer as I walked through the door. "Good morning, Mr. Deveraux. Did you have a merry Christmas?"

I offered her a smile. "I did, Kaylee, and you? Did Del get you that scarf you wanted?"

Her grin spread. "He did. And he gave me this too." She held out her hand and waggled her left finger, showing me a diamond solitaire.

"Well, then congratulations are in order. Del's not only a lucky man, but an intelligent one to boot."

A blush tinged her cheeks. "Thanks, Mr. Deveraux." She handed me a stack of messages.

I hoped it would be me and Rose walking down the aisle in the not-so-distant future, but I knew better than to push the issue. We hadn't been together long, but I knew I'd never find anyone else I'd rather spend the rest of my life with.

I pointed a thumb toward my office. "I need to make an important call, so I'd appreciate it if you'd hold my calls until I'm done."

"Of course, Mr. Deveraux."

I shut the door behind me and opened my laptop, then looked up the number for Skeeter Malcolm's pool hall and called it from my burner phone.

It was early, probably too early for him to be there, but rumor had it he was an early to work and late to leave kind of guy. The phone rang several times before it was answered. "Malcolm's Pool Hall."

"I'd like to speak to Skeeter Malcolm."

"And who's calling?"

I paused before answering. "Someone with some helpful information."

He hesitated. "Why don't you tell me what it is and I'll pass it on."

"I know you're trying to helpful, but I need to speak to Mr. Malcolm myself."

He chuckled. "Well, let me see if *Mr.* Malcolm is willing to talk to someone with helpful information."

I cringed. Damn, I should have actually come up with a plan before calling.

But to my surprise, Malcolm's voice came on the line. "What's so damned important you couldn't tell Jed?"

"Mr. Malcolm?"

"Skeeter Malcolm at your service." I heard the snicker in his voice.

"It's Mason Deveraux."

He laughed, not missing a beat. "Well, Mr. Mason Deveraux, I can't say I expected to hear from you. To what do I owe the honor of your call?"

"I have some information I think you'll find helpful."

"So you've said. The question is why you would want to help *me*."

I took a breath. "My duty is to ensure the safety of all Fenton County's citizens. Yourself included."

"You're insinuating I'm not safe."

"Well…" I drawled. "I could point out that you have more than enough enemies to be perpetually unsafe, but I know of one in particular who would like to see your demise. And I suspect you're not aware of this one."

"Why don't you tell me who it is and we'll see if I'm surprised."

"J.R. Simmons."

He paused. "The chief deputy's father?" He still kept his cool, but I could tell I'd caught him off guard.

"The one and the same."

"How'd I catch the attention of King Simmons?"

"I was hoping you could tell me."

He laughed. "You honestly think I'd tell you if I knew?"

"I'd give you full immunity."

"Why?" When I didn't answer, he continued, his voice harsher than I expected. "What's in it for you?"

"Like I said, I've got this penchant for keeping the county safe. And since you're a citizen of this county…" My voice trailed off.

"No. There's more to it."

The last thing I wanted to do was discuss Rose with Skeeter Malcolm. Especially after the way he'd looked at her when we ran into him at a restaurant a couple of weeks ago. "That's all I'm at liberty to tell you."

"Then thanks for the warning." He hung up and I stared at the blank cell phone screen. I'd gotten absolutely nothing from that call and wasn't likely to get anything else. I'd blown this one too.

I was really on a damn roll.

I stared at my computer screen, a tension headache brewing at the back of my neck. The DA wanted me out, particularly now that he knew I was on to his crooked ways, and J.R. knew I was sniffing around. I probably wouldn't have this job for long, which meant I couldn't afford to waste time. I might have to get my hands dirty to get things rolling. And while I'd promised to tell Rose what I'd discovered in Little Rock and anything else I was at liberty to tell, the dirty part didn't qualify.

I also needed a backup plan. Rose was just about to launch her new business, so she wasn't leaving Fenton County…and I wasn't leaving her. So I needed to figure out what I would do if I lost my job. And if it got to that point, I'd know I'd stumbled onto something important enough to make J.R. nervous. While I'd told Rose that murdering people wasn't in J.R. Simmons' wheelhouse, I wasn't so sure in this case.

I pulled my keys out of my pocket and unlocked my bottom drawer, reaching inside to pull a handgun out of the bottom drawer. I set the Glock on my desk and stared at it long and hard, a knife blade of worry working its way through my chest. After a dangerous incident in Little Rock, I'd always kept a gun in my office for protection, but I'd never had to use it.

I had a sickening feeling that would soon change.

Chapter Six

Rose

For the first time in months, I had felt lonely as I ate breakfast at my kitchen table. I'd spent most of my twenty-five years alone. Even now, I was used to being alone off and on during the day. But I'd gotten used to spending my mornings with Mason, so I'd stared at his empty chair with an ache in my heart. Not because I was sitting there with just Muffy for company. I could handle being alone. It was the way he'd left that morning.

I knew I was being unfair. Mason was risking his life and his career to protect me, and I had repaid him by getting upset and being ugly. Still, I wasn't some delicate flower that needed to be protected from the truth, and while I knew Mason well enough to know that he wasn't trying to insult my intelligence, I had to know what was going on. It was not just his life or mine, after all—it was *ours*.

So I breathed a sigh of relief when he called and apologized. I was even more relieved when he said he wanted to tell me what he could. Finally, we could work on this together.

I finished cleaning up the kitchen and herded Muffy into the truck to head into town. After the early freezing rain, I'd put off going into the office, preferring to wait for the temperature to warm up enough to make the roads safe. Besides, it was the holiday season and we weren't even open yet. But today was Neely Kate's first day and I was hoping to get there before she did.

Nevertheless, I wasn't surprised to find Bruce Wayne already at the office when I walked through the front door. He was bent over his computer with a frustrated grimace on his face.

"Hey, Bruce Wayne," I said as I shrugged off my coat.

Muffy raced over to him and put her paws on his legs. He grinned as he rubbed the back of her head, but he didn't answer me. I thought again about how reserved he'd been at Christmas dinner. Something was clearly wrong.

I tossed my coat on the desk and rolled my chair over to him, the sound of the wheels squeaking against the wood floor adding to the tension. "Why are you mad at me, Bruce Wayne? Is it because I went to New Orleans with Neely Kate last week and left you to go to that estate sale alone? I'm sorry. I shouldn't have gone."

His hands trembled as he pulled away from Muffy and sat up straighter in his chair. Bruce Wayne hated confrontation. "If I did everything while you sat on a throne of pillows, I'd never begrudge you for one second, Rose Gardner."

I leaned forward. "You know I'd never do such a thing, Bruce Wayne. We're partners and I haven't done my share in the craziness of the last few weeks. But I promise you, I won't slack off anymore."

He glanced up, his gaze guarded. "That's not why I'm mad you at you, Rose."

"Then what is it? I'm plum tired of getting the silent treatment from you."

His eyes hardened. "The Lady in Black."

My stomach tumbled to my feet. "What are you talkin' about?"

"You know darn good and well what I'm talking about."

"I…"

"Don't try to deny it, Rose. *I know.* I know you were with Skeeter last week at that meeting."

"How?" But of course he did. Lordy, I'd been stupid.

"Why?" he asked in a pained voice. "Why would you do it, Rose? And why didn't you tell me?"

I sighed. "I did it to protect you." Of course, that was exactly what Mason always said to me, so I knew it didn't offer a lick of comfort.

He shook his head, his eyes filled with hurt.

I rolled my chair closer. "Bruce Wayne, you can't be part of this. If you get caught up in any of it, you'll go back to prison. Maybe for good."

"Why did you do it at all?"

I sighed and leaned back in my chair. "Skeeter told me Mason's life was in danger. He promised to help protect him." He looked doubtful. "Mason's car accident wasn't an *accident*, Bruce Wayne. Someone tried to kill him."

He blinked in surprise. "What?"

"Joe said his brake lines had been cut." I lowered my voice. "But you can't tell anyone. They kept it from the public."

"Why would Skeeter want to protect Mason?"

I shrugged. "To get me to help him. Like you said, he knows how to get people to do what he wants."

"Okay. So he helped you and you helped him at this meeting. You're done."

"No, Bruce Wayne. I'm not." I licked my bottom lip. "I'm stuck for six more months."

"What? How?"

I cringed. "The fire at that strip club Gems. Mason was trapped inside. Skeeter saved Mason, but only after I agreed to help him for six months. But Mason has no idea Skeeter saved him and you can't breathe a word of it."

He walked to the window and looked out at the courthouse. "You have to tell Mason."

I gripped the arms of my desk chair. "I can't." My voice sounded small and afraid, even to me.

"He's gonna find out, Rose."

"Maybe not," I hedged. "I've kept it from him so far."

He didn't say anything, only kept looking out the window.

"I can do this, Bruce Wayne."

"Then let me help you."

I shook my head, adamant. "No. You can't be involved."

"I already *am* involved. I'm the one who got *you* involved."

We'd had this argument too many times to count. "I'm stuck in this mess. If you want to help me, the best thing you can do is help cover for me."

"Rose…"

"I can't tell Mason. It could ruin his career."

"It's gonna be worse when he finds out. Or if someone else finds out for him."

"Look, Skeeter was actually nice to me. Maybe I can convince him to let me off the hook."

He turned around and looked at me like I'd just announced I was gonna take up mud wrestling. "You can't seriously believe that."

No, but a girl could hope. "I don't want to talk about Skeeter Malcolm anymore."

He scowled, then sighed. "Fine. We can talk about another problem. I think we have enough equipment to handle bigger landscaping jobs now, but after I picked up the mower from the estate sale last week, I realized there's no way it'll all fit in the storage unit out back. It's in my garage for now, but I still need to pick up a few bigger pieces. We need something else."

"We can use the barn out on the farm."

"I got a flatbed trailer to cart the equipment to the job sites, but you're gonna have to pull the trailer around with your truck. My car won't do it."

"Sounds like you need a truck," I said.

"I can't afford a truck, Rose."

"You don't have to afford a truck, Bruce Wayne. The business would pay for it and it's a good idea…"

"Only we can't afford it. We've shot the wad on the front-end loader. We've got too much money going out, and none coming in."

He was right.

His cheeks flushed, a sure sign he didn't want to discuss the next subject, but he plunged ahead anyway.

"You know I think Neely Kate workin' here is a good idea, but how are we gonna pay her?"

I'd wondered the same thing. "I'll just pay her out of my paycheck."

He shook his head. "That's not fair to you. If we're partners, we should split the difference."

"Bruce Wayne, the farm is free and clear with no mortgage, and Mason is pulling more than his half in terms of our living expenses. You need all you're making to pay your rent and utilities."

"It doesn't seem right."

"I was the one to suggest that she work for us. I should have consulted you first, so it's more than fair for me to cover her salary. And if it bugs you too much, you can pay me back when we're in the black."

"Or we can ask Joe to help."

"No," I said with more force than I'd intended. "We won't be asking Joe for anything. This is *our* business. He may be part of the nursery side, but he has nothin' to do with this part."

He held up his hands. "Okay, fair enough."

"She's gonna come in soon. Now, I don't want her to know that we're cash poor."

He chuckled. "She ain't stupid. She already knows we're cash poor, and even if she didn't, she'll figure it out within about five minutes if she's any kind of bookkeeper at all."

The front door opened and Neely Kate burst in. "Good morning!"

I grinned at her. It was true that I should have consulted Bruce Wayne before hiring my best friend as our bookkeeper, receptionist, and anything else we needed her for. Nevertheless, I wasn't sorry. She was one of the best things to have come into my life since my momma's murder.

But then again, from the way Bruce Wayne was beaming, I doubt he would have put up much of a fuss.

"Neely Kate!" I hopped out of my chair and gave her a big hug. "Welcome to your first day at RBW Landscaping!"

She squeezed me before pulling loose. "Are you gonna greet me like that every day? Because if you are, I hope I see you at the office *before* you start digging in people's yards when summer comes around."

I laughed. "I'll keep that in mind. How was your Christmas?"

She lifted her eyebrows in mock disgust. "Well, I got more pickled beets and okra than anyone has a right to enjoy." She opened her purse and dug around, then pulled out a package wrapped in brown paper. "But I thought Bruce Wayne might like this one."

He reached up and hesitantly took the package. "What is it?"

"Raccoon jerky. My Aunt Thelma made it. She's known around the county for her—"

"Jerky. I know about Thelma's jerky." His face lit up like she'd given him a bar of gold rather than strips of dried raccoon meat. "Her jerky's hard to come by."

"Well, now you have some," Neely Kate said with a grin.

His smile faded. "I didn't get you a Christmas gift."

"It ain't a Christmas gift." She shrugged. "Consider it a thanks-for-lettin'-me-work-for-you present."

I bumped her arm. "Where's mine?"

She gave me an ornery grin. "Why, I thought the sheer joy of having me in the office should be enough for *you.* I was worried that Bruce Wayne might need a little convincin'."

He shook his head. "I'm glad you're goin' to be workin' here, Neely Kate. All I ask is that you and Rose keep all that women stuff to yourselves."

"You mean birthin' babies and such?" she teased with an exaggerated country drawl.

He cringed. "Yeah."

"Then I'll try not to let my water break here at work."

He ducked his head to hide his blush. "That'd be much appreciated."

Neely Kate winked at me and I shook my head. I could already see that these two were gonna be a handful together. But my heart warmed with happiness.

Since Neely Kate didn't have a desk yet, we set her up at mine. She didn't waste any time opening the accounting program and entering in information for both the nursery and the landscaping office.

I grabbed a notebook and moved over to the table we'd set up in the back for possible client meetings. Both the nursery and the landscaping business were gonna have an opening and I needed to finalize the logistics. But truth be told, I really needed to plan it with my sister.

Releasing a frustrated groan, I stood. "I'm gonna go check on Violet at the nursery."

Both Bruce Wayne and Neely Kate looked up in surprise.

I lifted a shoulder in a half shrug. "What? We need to finalize a reopening plan, and I want to check on how the reorganizing's goin'."

Neely Kate pointed a red and white striped fingernail at me. "Don't you be lettin' her talk you into spendin' a ton of money on it. There isn't much left to spare."

I glanced over at Bruce Wayne, who was grinning like the cat that got the cream. Okay, so he'd been right. I grabbed my coat and slipped my arms into the sleeves. "Don't worry. I won't. I don't see the point of putting too much effort into it either, but we have to do something."

My gaze moved over to Muffy, who was asleep in her dog bed. "Do y'all mind if I leave Muffy here? I'm meeting Mason for lunch at Merilee's at noon."

Neely Kate waggled her eyebrows. "A lunch date? And we're not invited?"

My shoulders tensed. "Not this time."

"I was teasing," she said. "But now you have me worried about what's goin' on."

Bruce Wayne's eyes narrowed with suspicion.

"Nothin'." I waved my hand in dismissal. "We're just gonna talk about…things." That was not gonna appease my friends, but it was the best I could come up with at the moment. And I sure couldn't tell them about J.R. Simmons.

"Is Mason upset about what happened in New Orleans?" Neely Kate asked.

"He was upset, but not in the way you think. I think he was more upset that we got into trouble and he wasn't there to help."

"Then what's goin' on?"

I rolled my eyes. This was definitely gonna be one of the perils of working so close to Neely Kate. I would have to tell her about my indentured service to Skeeter, but not today. Especially since it had nothing to do with this situation. "Did it ever occur to you that we were separated all last week and had lots of family and friends around over Christmas and maybe we just want a chance to spend some time alone?"

Neely Kate studied me for a moment. "No. If you were lookin' for that kind of alone time, you would be *eatin' lunch*—" she used air quotes, "—in Mason's office."

Bruce Wayne blushed.

I shook my head and laughed. "I think I'll leave you to your imagination because it's way more exciting than what's really goin' on." I opened the front door and walked out into the late December day, hoping I hadn't just told a big fat lie.

Chapter Seven
Joe

After Mason left, I sat behind the old Sinclair gas station for a good five minutes, replaying the conversation in my head and debating whether to call him and tell him that he was still in danger. I decided to sit on the decision for the moment. Mason likely knew, anyway, and I didn't feel up to dealing with him after the way our talk had ended.

I drove away from the gas station without knowing where I was headed. I was moving into the farmhouse out by Rose this week, but there wasn't much to pack. Most of my things were still in my old apartment in Little Rock, not because I planned to move back there, but because that life felt like a million years ago. I wasn't ready to face the specter of my old self yet.

I'd made this move to Henryetta mostly to win Rose back, but I also felt something here that I hadn't found anywhere else—a sense of belonging. There was the potential for me to make a real difference here, and my father was going to ruin it, just like everything else in my life. There had to be a way out of this situation that would allow me to do my job without endangering Rose, but I'd be damned if I'd figured it out yet.

Suddenly I knew where I needed to go, though I didn't question the irony of my destination until I parked at the curb in front of her house. After I got a couple of parts and my toolbox out of the trunk, I headed up to the front porch to ring the bell.

Maeve Deveraux opened the door wearing a ruffly apron and a warm smile. The house smelled inviting—like sugar and spice and something warm baking in the oven. Then again, it always seemed to smell that way. "Good morning, Joe! Happy Day after Christmas."

"I hope I'm not here too early."

She stepped back and opened the door wider. "Don't be silly. You know I'm an early riser. The question is what are you doing out so early on such a dreary day?"

I stepped through the front door. "I had an early meeting that didn't last as long as expected, so I thought I'd make good use of the time and fix the pipe under your sink. I got the part I needed."

She shut the door behind me as I headed into the kitchen. "You know you don't have to do this, Joe. I could just hire a handyman. I feel badly about not paying you."

I set my toolbox on the floor in front of the sink and patted my stomach. "You pay me, Maeve. Good food is worth more than gold to a bachelor like myself."

She waved her hand. "Please. I have it on good authority that you're a great cook."

My eyes widened in surprise. "Really? Where'd you hear that?"

She paused and broke into a soft smile. "Why, from Rose."

I swallowed, riding out the stab of pain in my heart. "She talks about me?"

"You were an important part of her life, Joe. Of course she talks about you."

I glanced out the window over the sink, then back at her, surprised she was telling me this. "What does she say?"

"She says you're a wonderful cook and she's gotten out of the habit because of you. She's quite self-conscious about it, actually. I do a lot of the cooking when we get together, and she was worried I would think her incapable of making a meal. But she cooked most of Christmas dinner yesterday despite my insistence on helping. She made a lasagna, so it wasn't a typical Christmas dinner."

I chuckled. "She made a lasagna." Leave it to Rose to make something non-traditional. But it only made the ache in my chest more intense. "I'm sure it was delicious. Don't let her fool you. I may have done most of the cooking when we were together, but whenever she did cook, I'd have to fit in extra workouts because of all the helpings I'd eat."

"I believe it." She moved to the oven and turned on the light, revealing a pan inside. "And speaking of food, I'm baking a batch of cinnamon rolls that should be out in a few minutes. You'll have one, of course."

I opened the cabinet beneath the sink and dropped to the floor. "You spoil me, Maeve. So let's call it even." I looked up at her. "You haven't told Rose I'm helping you out, have you?"

Her lips pressed together before she answered. "No. I've respected your request for privacy. I haven't told anyone."

"Thank you." I wasn't sure what Rose would think about me helping Mason's mother. Would she assume I was spying on her? Trying to worm my way even deeper into her life? Whatever the case, I was positive Mason would presume I was up to something. And honestly, I could see why he might think that. Maeve Deveraux had a good heart. I was fairly sure she was incapable of forming enemies, if only for the fact that she was so kind to me, the man who was partially responsible for the murder of her daughter. Savannah's death still weighed heavily on my conscience, so when I realized Maeve had some odd jobs that needed doing around the house, I showed up with my toolbox one day and spent an hour or so taking care of them. It had been the first of several visits.

I'd be lying if I didn't admit that I felt a smug sense of satisfaction that I was doing something for Mason's mother that he couldn't. It was just further proof that he couldn't give Rose what she needed. And while I still believed that, it wasn't my primary motivation for helping her. I genuinely liked Maeve. She reminded me a lot of Roberta, our housekeeper when I was a boy.

I set to work on replacing the PVC elbow of the drain while she puttered around the kitchen, softly humming as she worked. When I stood and ran some water to make sure the new joint didn't leak, she set a warm frosted cinnamon roll and a fork on a plate for me.

"I hope you have time to stay and eat with me today," she said as she put the plate on her small kitchen table, across from an identical one.

I turned the water off and hesitated. I was tempted. Very tempted. But I wondered about the intelligence of spending more time with her than was necessary to do repairs. I was pressing my luck as it was. "I need to get back to…"

"Poppycock," she said in a good-natured tone. "You can spare ten minutes. I want to hear about your Christmas."

I snorted. "I assure you, you *don't* want to hear about Christmas with my family."

Her eyebrows rose with a playful look. "Now I *really* want to hear it." She grabbed a couple of coffee cups out of the cabinet and filled them before setting them next to the plates. "Did I mention I make the best cinnamon rolls in the state of Arkansas?"

A warm laugh rumbled in my chest. "I'm sure my old housekeeper Roberta would have a thing or two to say about that."

"Then sit down, and you can be the judge."

I tilted my head to the side and grinned at her. "It's hard to turn down a challenge like that."

"Then have a seat." I did, and she took the seat across from me.

After several bites, I murmured my appreciation. "I think you might have an honest claim to that cinnamon roll title."

She grinned and took a sip of her coffee. "So your housekeeper made you cinnamon rolls?"

I sliced my fork through the gooey baked good. "Roberta was our housekeeper, but she was more than that. I never officially had a nanny, but she pretty much raised me. And while we had someone who cooked when my parents entertained—which was a lot—Roberta was more into comfort food. She could always tell when my sister Kate or I was having a bad day, and she'd make our favorites to cheer us up."

"Are you close with Kate? I don't think I've heard you mention her before."

"No." I took a bite of the roll to stall. I wasn't sure I should tell her anything about my family, but for some reason it felt right. "In fact, I hadn't seen her for two years until she showed up unexpectedly for Christmas dinner yesterday."

"So it was a family reunion?"

I gave her a wry grin. "Of a sort." When she gave me a questioning glance, I continued. "My parents weren't expecting her either, and Kate has always had a mind of her own. My parents can't control her, which means they don't know how to handle her."

"Why do you think that is?"

I picked up my coffee cup. "She doesn't care about anyone or anything, so my parents have nothing to leverage over her. She's untouchable."

"You don't really believe that, do you?"

I took a sip of coffee. "We hadn't heard from her in two years. That sounds pretty untouchable to me. And trust me, if my parents could figure out how to force her to toe the line, they'd do it."

"But is she happy?"

My eyebrows rose. "*That* is a good question. I intended to talk to her and find out what she's been doing, but my father insisted we have a chat before I left." I'd been so aggravated by my conversation with my father, I'd left before I'd had a chance to talk to her. But I needed to steer this conversation in a different direction because there was no way we were going down that path. "Hilary was there with her parents, and Kate had a field day with her."

Maeve paused, then asked, "Your old girlfriend?"

"Go ahead and say it—the mother of my unborn child? Yes. Hilary's parents have been close friends with mine since before we were born. We all grew up together, and Kate and Hilary's mutual animosity goes back to our early childhood. Hilary and I are the same age and Kate's two years younger. Hilary always saw Kate as competition, and Kate was more than happy to accept the challenge."

"So it was an entertaining day, I take it?" She chuckled. "And here you said it wasn't exciting."

"Kate's one of the few people who can get under Hilary's skin. That was indeed fun to watch."

"I take it that you don't get along well with the mother of your child."

I sighed. "We have a very complicated relationship."

"I'm not judging, Joe. Just trying to understand."

Oddly enough, I believed her. "Hilary's like a crutch. A very bad habit. It just took me too long to realize that. I was weak after I was forced to leave Rose and Hilary took advantage of that fact." I realized my error as soon as the words left my mouth. Would she pick up on the meaning behind what I'd said, or did she—like most people probably did—think I'd purposely left Rose behind to chase my supposed dream of running for political office?

Maeve went in a totally different direction. "So you're sure the baby's yours?" She looked pained to ask.

I was silent for a moment. "I'll insist upon paternity testing, but yeah, I'll be shocked if the baby isn't mine."

"But you don't plan to marry her?"

"No."

She waved her hand in dismissal. "If you don't love her, that's for the best. Many a marriage has begun with an unplanned pregnancy only to end in a disastrous divorce later. Then the poor child gets caught in the chaos. It's a new day and age, and it's much more acceptable now for parents to remain unmarried. As long as you're a good father to your baby, that's the important thing, right?"

I didn't have an answer as to what would happen after the baby came. I still struggled to wrap my head around the idea. Would I be a good father? My own parents hadn't been the best role models. I knew part of the reason I was balking was because Rose wasn't the baby's mother. All my dreams of having a baby had been with her, and I still couldn't let go.

Maeve leaned closer. "You know Hilary's telling everyone you're engaged?"

I released a heavy breath. "I suspected. It's never going to happen."

She watched me for a moment, then said quietly, "I know you don't love Hilary, but is part of your reason for not wanting to marry her that you still hold out hope for you and Rose?"

I sucked in a deep breath and let it out. Rose could see the future; could Mason's mother read minds? I cleared my throat. "I'm not sure we should be having this conversation."

She reached out a hand and covered mine. "I know you still love her." When I started to protest, she smiled softly. "It's written all over your face whenever you talk about her. You can't hide it."

"Maeve..."

"If you still love Rose, then it's only further confirmation that you shouldn't marry Hilary."

I gaped at her. "But wouldn't it solve a pesky problem for Mason if I did? If I were married to Hilary, I'd be out of the way."

"It's not that easy, Joe, and you know it." She sat back in her chair and seemed to consider her next words carefully. "Rose Gardner is an intelligent woman who is capable of making up her own mind. Trying to keep someone who wants to be somewhere else is like trying to hold sand in an open hand. Your love for Rose has no bearing on Mason. It's only Rose's feelings that need concern you."

I wasn't sure how to answer. It wasn't what I'd expected her to say.

"I know you don't want to hear this, and perhaps I'm biased since I'm Mason's mother, but Rose seems very happy to me. I think you need to ask yourself if you want to possess Rose...or if you want her to be happy."

I set my fork on the table. "I think I should be goin' now."

She stood as I did. "Joe, Rose feels how she feels. How *you* feel can't change that."

I paused and stared out the window, a familiar ache filling my chest. "I know."

"Sometimes you have to let something go and if it's meant to be, it will happen."

"What do you think I'm doin'?"

She gave me a warm smile. "I think you're doin' the best you can. You're hurting, but you need to figure out how to take that pain away without relying on her, because I think you were hurting long before you met Rose." She patted my arm. "You need to figure out how to live the best possible life you can without her, and if she happens to change her mind at some point, you'll be a much stronger man when she comes back to you. Or for the next woman who claims your heart."

A lump filled my throat and I tilted my head as I watched her. "Why are you so nice to me? I want to steal your son's girlfriend."

She shook her head. "I'm nice to you because you are a good person, Joe Simmons, and I can't stand to see you so lost. You just need to find your way."

A good person? I definitely didn't think it was true, but Rose had always told me I was. Now Maeve was telling me the same thing. Could there be some truth to it after all? "Find my way… Without Rose, I'm not even sure where to go."

"I'm not so sure about that. You like your work in the sheriff's department. And you're moving out to that farmhouse so you can restore it. You're *already* on the right path. Fill your life with things you love and love will find you, whether it's with Rose or someone else."

But I couldn't imagine a life without Rose, and I wasn't ready to consider loving anyone else. Maybe I'd never be.

"You just need to take it one day at a time."

"Of course you're telling me to move on without her," I said stubbornly. "You don't want her to leave Mason."

"Joe." Her tone hardened as her gaze penetrated mine. "If Rose loves *you*, then I would rather that she rip out Mason's heart than marry him. I've seen too many loveless marriages make everyone involved miserable, which is exactly why I said you shouldn't marry Hilary." She paused and her voice softened. "I confess that I *do* hope Mason and Rose get married someday. Considering the short time I've known her, I love Rose more than I ever would have expected. But I only want that if they truly love each other."

"I have to go." I started to walk past her, but she grabbed my arm and held tight.

"I've overstepped my bounds and I'm so sorry, but I can't stand to see the pain in your eyes, Joe. I want you to be happy."

"Even after I killed your daughter." The words came out before I could think on them. But the statement had been threatening to burst out of me for some time now.

Her hold tightened. "You know I don't for one minute believe that, so we won't have that particular conversation, but *you* obviously still need to find a way to let *that* go too."

She was right, but I wasn't sure how.

She looked up into my eyes and smiled softly. "I hope you come back and see me again. I would really miss your visits if you were to stay away." Her grin turned mischievous and she winked. "I promise to keep my conversation to the weather and the local bingo hall gossip."

I looked down at the floor and grinned. "As chief deputy sheriff, that bingo gossip could come in handy."

"Good. It's settled. You'll come back for a visit." She wrapped her arms around my back and gave me a squeeze.

I squeezed her back, then picked up my toolbox. "You still won't tell—"

"*No one* knows you come visit me, but not because I'm ashamed of our friendship. I understand why you feel the way you do, so I respect your decision."

"Thank you." Maybe I was stupid to believe her. She could feed Mason everything I told her, but I couldn't believe the kind woman in front of me was capable of it. "I need to get goin'."

"It's going to be cold and wet today. You keep bundled up."

I grinned. She reminded me so much of Roberta it made my heart ache. "Will do. Let me know if something else comes up with the house before I show up for my next visit."

I was surprised to see the tears glistening in her eyes as she smiled at me. "I will. And I look forward to it."

I left her warm house for the cold rain that was now falling. I'd barely made it out of her neighborhood when my phone rang. I wasn't surprised to see it was the sheriff's department.

"I'm on my way in now," I said as I answered.

"That's good, sir," the front desk receptionist said. "Because there's a woman who insists that she see you."

"Who is it?"

"She won't say, but she says she's not leaving until she's said her piece."

I wasn't in the mood to deal with disgruntled county citizens. "Isn't the sheriff in yet? Hand her off to him."

"She insists on *you.*"

"Great," I grumbled, wondering whom I'd pissed off this time and why. "I should be there in fifteen minutes. But since I have you, can you patch me through to Deputy Miller"

"Sure."

Moments later, Deputy Miller answered.

"Miller, I have a special job for you, but I want you to keep it between us."

"Of course, sir."

"I think Mason Deveraux is still in danger, but I'd prefer not to make it widespread knowledge in the department. I'd like for you to keep tabs on him periodically throughout the day. If you discover anything suspicious, you answer directly to me."

"Do you have any idea who has it out for him?"

"No. I'm hoping you'll be able find something for me."

"I'll do my best, sir."

I knew he would. He was probably one of the most dependable men on the force. I still needed to tell Mason, so I pulled into a parking lot and sent him a quick text.

I'm not certain the threat to your safety is eliminated. If you notice anything out of the ordinary, let me know. I've got Miller monitoring you so don't be surprised if you see him in the background.

I wondered if I should tell him more, but other than knowing my father was involved, there wasn't anything else to tell. Mason knowing about my father wouldn't keep him any safer.

The streets of Henryetta were emptier than usual, most likely because the citizens were worried about icy roads, so

I made it to the sheriff's office quickly. When I entered the lobby, I wasn't prepared to see the woman sitting across the room from me, grinning at me like she was up to nothing but trouble.

My sister Kate.

Chapter Eight
Joe

Hello, big brother," she said, getting to her feet and adjusting her purse strap on her shoulder. She wore jeans covered with holes, a flannel shirt and a tan jacket.

"I'm surprised to see you here." It was an understatement.

"After your meeting with dear old Dad, you ran out of the house like a man on fire. We didn't get a chance to have our little chat."

I shifted my weight. "You never thought to pick up your phone and call me? You could have easily gotten the number from Mom."

"Nah, I prefer a face-to-face meeting."

I glanced toward the door leading to the back offices. I knew I didn't have anything pressing waiting on me and I was still a bit early for my shift. I could take Kate back to my office, but I preferred to keep the Simmons family chaos as far from my work life as possible. "Judy," I said to the receptionist behind the glass partition. "I'm going out for a bit. Call me if you need me."

She barely glanced up. "Will do."

"Have you had breakfast?" I asked my sister, gesturing to the door.

Kate followed me out to the parking lot. "No. Are you going to take me to some quaint Podunk restaurant?"

I stopped and turned to face her, my back muscles tight. "I live in this town and county. If you are bringing our parents' small-minded attitude with you, just get back in your car and drive back to wherever it is you came from. Because I'm not putting up with it."

She held up her hands in defense, a sly grin spreading across her face. "Down, boy. I didn't mean it like it sounded. Sometimes the snark slips out unchecked."

I gave her a brisk nod. "Okay."

"But I really do want to eat at a small-town restaurant with down-home cooking. Like Roberta used to make."

I watched her for a second. She hadn't mentioned Roberta since she left when we were teens. What was she up to? "We can go to Merilee's in the town square. They make great pancakes and waffles."

"Sounds great to me."

I gestured to my sheriff's cruiser behind me. "I'm technically on duty, so we better take separate cars."

"Don't want your sister sitting in a police car, tarnishing the Simmons name?" she sneered.

"No, there's a chance I'll get called in. If that happens, I don't want to leave you stranded."

"Oh."

I pushed out a heavy breath. "Look, I appreciate that you drove out here, but maybe you should just go." I wanted to talk to her, but I didn't like her here on my turf. The truth was, I didn't trust her. Until I knew she wasn't up to trouble, I wanted her as far away from my new life as possible. I'd just arrange to talk to her on more neutral territory.

Her cockiness slipped away and she gave me a genuine smile. "No. I really do want to see you. Sorry. Old habits are too easy to fall back into."

Hilary came to mind. "Tell me about it."

She cocked her head and winked. "I promise to be on my best behavior, and if I do misbehave, you can put me in jail."

I shook my head and grinned. "That seems like an excessive punishment."

"Then come up with your own. I really want blueberry pancakes. Tell me this Merry's place makes blueberry pancakes."

I laughed. "Merilee's makes fantastic blueberry pancakes…not at good as mine, but pretty doggone good anyway."

"Nobody likes a braggart." But I noticed she didn't correct me. She'd tasted my pancakes when we were teenagers.

"Just follow me."

"Yes, sir," she said with a salute.

I sighed. "I have a feeling I'm going to regret this." And as I drove to the Henryetta town square, I already did. My life in Fenton County was my Joe McAllister world. Hilary had already botched that by renting a house close to the courthouse, but now my sister was here too. I might have felt better about the whole thing if I knew what she was after, but she was a total wild card. We hadn't gotten along for years, and her entire mission in life had always been to aggravate our parents and Hilary. Given everything she'd said the day before, I wondered if she was here to stoke my rebellion as another act of defiance.

I pulled into a parking space on the square, casting a quick glance at the RBW Landscaping office across the street. Rose's truck was parked in front of it and I felt a pull to go see her. But Kate had already gotten out of her small car and was walking toward me. She looked over her shoulder to see what had captured my attention, and the last thing I wanted to do was have *that* conversation with her.

"Let's see how good your Merilee's actually is." She looped her arm through mine and we walked into the warm restaurant together. The hostess seated us by the window, which seemed to delight Kate, if the grin on her face was any indication. We slipped off our coats as the waitress walked over.

"Good morning, Chief Deputy Simmons," she said with a warm smile. "What can I get for you and…" She glanced over at Kate.

I had no intention of filling in the blank. The less this town knew about my family, the better. And once word got out that my sister had been here for a visit, it would be a subject for all the gossips. But Kate had other ideas.

She glanced up at the waitress, her eyes sparkling with mischief. "Kate. I'm just dropping by to check up on my big brother."

The waitress looked relieved. "How nice to meet you, Ms. Simmons."

"Just Kate. And I would love a cup of coffee, *Bonnie*." She read off the poor girl's nametag, then turned to me. "Joe?"

Bonnie glanced down at me. "Deputy Simmons, do you want your usual coffee and juice?"

"Yeah, that would be great, Bonnie." She nodded and smiled before walking away.

"You have a usual," Kate said, lifting an eyebrow. "So you're a regular here?"

"It's a small town and I spend a lot of time at the courthouse. Not to mention the food is good."

She held up her hands and leaned back in her chair. "No need to get so defensive. I was just asking."

Bringing her here had been a huge mistake. "What are you doing in Henryetta, anyway, Kate?" I asked, sounding tired.

"I'm hoping to eat blueberry pancakes if Bonnie ever comes back with my coffee and your *usual*."

"You can get blueberry pancakes anywhere. Why are you here harassing me?"

Her smile fell. "Is that how you see this? Me harassing you?"

I placed my forearms on the table and leaned toward her, lowering my voice. "Look, you left two years ago after making my life hell and letting me know you were done with me and the rest of our family, so you can't be surprised if I'm a bit suspicious."

Her lips twisted as she seemed to consider my statement. "Fair enough," she finally said. "But I assure you that I come in peace."

"Forgive me if I reserve judgment on that."

"Challenge accepted."

Her statement made me trust her less. My sister considered everything in life a challenge or a game. The real question was what she hoped to gain at the end of this particular "challenge," because I sure as hell had a hard time believing it was me.

Bonnie came back and set a cup of coffee in front of Kate and a coffee and a glass of orange juice in front of me. "Are you two ready to order?"

I poured creamer into my coffee. I'd had a cinnamon roll at Maeve's, but this day was already turning out to be crap. I could use more comfort food. "I'll take fried eggs and a side of bacon."

Kate leaned forward, her eyes sparkling. "I hear you make exceptional blueberry pancakes."

Bonnie grinned. "I don't personally make them, but Glenn does a pretty decent job."

"Then give me an order of those with a side of bacon."

"Gave up the vegan stage?" I asked.

Kate gave me a withering glare. "You saw me eat turkey yesterday."

"You're presuming I paid attention to what you ate," I countered, even though I had noticed.

Bonnie laughed. "You sound like me and my brother. We bicker like cats and dogs, but if someone messes with us, we're the first ones to come to each other's defense."

After Bonnie disappeared into the kitchen, I glanced at Kate and realized she was staring at me with a strange expression.

"What?" I asked as I picked up my coffee.

"Why aren't you and I like that?" The words sounded more serious than anything she'd said since showing up at our parents' house the previous day.

I took a sip, then put the cup down. "Maybe because you always hated my guts."

"I did not."

I shrugged. "Typically the older sibling finds the younger one annoying. The roles were reversed in our case."

She was quiet for several seconds.

"Why are you here, Kate?"

"I told you."

"You wanted to chat." I sat back in my chair and crossed my arms over my chest. "Let's start with you. Two years ago I tried calling you, only to discover your phone was disconnected. Then I stopped by your apartment, and your roommate said you'd moved out. I stopped by the shop where you worked and your boss told me you'd quit. No forwarding address. You didn't even pick up your last paycheck." I sat upright and put my hands on the table. "Who does that?"

Her eyes filled with defiance and she shrugged. "Someone who wants a fresh start."

"I filed a damned missing person's report on you, Kate."

"I bet Mom and Dad loved that," she sneered. "Their ne'er-do-well daughter makes the trashy tabloids."

"Don't flatter yourself. It barely made the news."

"After a little Simmons intervention, no doubt."

I didn't deny it, although I'd had no part in it. "Last summer I ran into one of your friends who told me you'd gone out to California."

She lifted her eyebrows and said, "You really are a detective."

"Cut the shit, Kate. Why did you run off to California?"

A twisted smile lifted her lips. "I was just following the example set by the Beverly Hillbillies. Arkansas family makes good on oil, then runs off to the land of the beautiful."

The only way she was going to give me an answer was if she wanted to. As I'd learned long ago, Katherine Elizabeth Simmons could not be forced to do anything she didn't want to do.

"So what have you been doing out there?"

Her shoulders seemed to relax and the hint of a grin lifted the corners of her mouth. "A little of this and a little of that. But that's all behind me now."

"That's specific."

She winked. "I'm not sure an officer of the law would appreciate what I've been up to."

"Taking after our father's footsteps?"

Her face hardened. "What's that supposed to mean?"

I shook my head. "Never mind. So you left California. What are you up to now?"

"I'm still trying to figure out my next move." She poured sugar into her coffee cup and waved her hand toward me. "So you gave up all the prestige of being a detective for the Arkansas State Police to become a deputy sheriff in Fenton County." Derision laced her words. "And when I say working for the state police was prestigious, you have to know it's little better than a step up from garbage removal."

"And you ask why we aren't close," I said dryly.

"Hey, for most people, I'm sure it's perfectly wonderful. But you're a Simmons." She narrowed her eyes. "*Groomed for greatness.*"

"Nobody asked me if I wanted that life. It was just presumed I'd live it."

"I don't recall you putting up much of a fuss."

My pulse pounded in my head. I really didn't want to have this conversation. I spread out my arms and looked her in the eye. "Take a good look. This is what it looks like to slum it in Fenton County. Now that you've had your laugh at my expense, you can leave."

"Don't be so defensive."

"You're insulting where I *live* and what I do."

She patted my hand on the table. "Okay. Okay. I get it. No insulting anything in Fenton County, no matter how hard it is to resist." She cocked her head. "Please tell me that does *not* include Hilary, since she claims to live here too now."

I had to stop my grin. "I think we can make an exception for her."

"Thank God."

Bonnie returned with our food and I was thankful for the reprieve. The sooner this meal ended, the better.

As Bonnie moved on to another table, Kate asked, "So what brought you here in the first place?"

"It sounds like you already know. I was undercover in Daniel Crocker's garage posing as a mechanic." Then I remembered something she'd said to Hilary. "You said Hilary messed up the report. How did she mess it up, and how do you know about it?"

She gave me a cocky grin, obviously pleased to have the upper hand again. "You didn't read it?"

"I gave my statement."

"But Hil-Monster was in charge of the entire thing. She left off a ton of information …information that put a certain someone in danger when Crocker broke out of prison."

The blood drained from my head. "*Rose?*"

"Yeah, Rose Gardner." She snapped her fingers. "You know her, don't you?"

"Cut the crap, Kate. I don't have time for your bullshit. How did she put Rose in danger?"

She picked up her fork and sliced into her pancakes. "She left things out of the report."

"You said that already. What kind of things?"

"Details about Rose's interactions with Crocker. The extent of her relationship with you. The police and sheriff's department didn't have the full information. The reason they didn't adequately protect her in the beginning was because they underestimated Crocker's obsession with her."

I shook my head. "How do you know this?"

"I have my sources."

"Who?" I repeated through clenched teeth.

"All you need to know is that I have connections. My connections fill me in on things that pertain to you. I caught wind of this little drama and started to do a little digging."

"Why the hell would you be interested in anything to do with me?"

She shot me a look of disgust. "Don't look so surprised. I'm your sister. It's my job to care."

"If you went out to California in the hopes of breaking into Hollywood, this little performance explains why you're back."

She laughed, a genuine laugh that caught the attention of the other restaurant patrons. "You really have changed. You're not the prick you were when I left."

"Didn't you leave off *arrogant?* That was always one of your favorite insults."

She took a bite of her bacon. "Nope, that part still seems to fit."

This was my second conflict of the day, third if I counted the tense part of my conversation with Maeve. This would have been a record for me even back in my hardass days, and I was weary of all the contention. She was right. I was a different man. I wanted peace and contentment now; I craved it. The realization startled me.

But at the moment, it was vital for me to find out what Kate knew and how she knew it. "You said Hilary changed the report."

"More like made it very abbreviated."

"And doing that put Rose in danger." I'd never looked at the full report, only my own portion of it. It had never occurred to me that I needed to check. But I planned to get a copy the first chance I got.

Kate studied me for a moment. "Tell me about your relationship with Rose Gardner."

"This sounds oddly like an interrogation."

She grinned, but it was a forced expression. "Humor me."

My jaw tensed. "Why? It sounds like you have it all figured out."

"Joe." Her tone softened. "I really want to hear about Rose."

I picked up my coffee cup and shook my head. "No. I'm not talking about her."

"Joe…"

"*No.*"

"Okay…" she drawled. "No discussing Rose. But tell me this: Do you plan to marry Hilary?"

"God, no."

"She doesn't believe that."

"Hilary can believe whatever deluded fantasy she chooses to. But that particular one will never turn into reality."

"And the baby is yours? You're sure of it? You know that Hil-Monster wouldn't blink an eye about passing someone else's fetus off as yours if she thought there was a chance you'd put a ring on it."

"She doesn't need me to put a ring on it," I said, my voice tense. "She got her own damn ring which she continues to wear. I'm sure you noticed yesterday. And the baby's mine. I'm going to insist on a paternity test after the baby's born, and she knows it. She's not sloppy enough to play pretend with something like this."

"And you're positive she's pregnant?"

"I went to the doctor and saw the baby's heartbeat on her ultrasound. She's pregnant, all right."

"But—"

"Kate, enough," I said. "If you're trying to find a loophole out of this mess that I've made, there isn't one. Trust me, I've spent plenty of sleepless nights trying to find it." I leveled my gaze. "And I might add that I find it creepy that you're taking on Dad's role of trying to get me out of trouble."

She laughed. "Yeah, I'm not comfortable in it either, but I can't let Hilary get away with trapping you like this."

Was that her purpose? To best Hilary? If so, I should jump on that bandwagon. But the truth was, though she was by all appearances a rebel, Kate was a Simmons through and through. I didn't trust her any more than I trusted our parents. I took several breaths, then lowered my voice. "Hilary and I slept together more than once around the time of the baby's conception. I was a willing participant, so the best thing I can do is accept responsibility for it and figure out how to make it work."

She took a bite of her bacon, keeping her gaze on me. "You've changed."

"Of course I have. You haven't seen me in two years. And besides, you already said I wasn't the prick I used to be."

She shook her head. "No. It's more than that. It's like you've grown up."

"About damn time, don't you think?" I grumbled.

"She did this," she whispered.

"Hilary?" I scoffed. "She'd rather I act like a child so she can control me. She's an enabler."

"No. Not Hilary. Rose."

My fork dropped out of my hand and clanged on my plate. "I will not discuss Rose with you."

"Okay," she said softly. "I'm sorry. I had no idea she meant so much to you."

"I'm just full of surprises," I grunted.

"Like the fact you're a part owner of a landscaping nursery. I had no idea you wanted to be a business owner."

How much did she know about my life? "Neither did I until it fell in my lap."

"Do you like it?"

"Hard to say," I said as I pushed the last piece of egg onto my fork. "The store was vandalized before Thanksgiving, and we haven't even reopened yet."

"When's the reopening?"

"Next week." I looked into her face. "You accused Hilary of purposely screwing up the report. Why would she do that?"

She put a hand on her chest and gave me a look of mock innocence. "Why are you asking me? You should be asking the mother of your baby."

There it was, the proof that my life was just a game with her…that she wasn't here to make nice with me and be my sister. If she really cared, she'd tell me everything she knew instead or parcel it out as she saw fit. I pulled out my wallet and looked for some cash. "It's been great catching up, but I have to get back to work." I set several bills on the table and stood.

"Sure, we'll talk more later."

I glared at her. "No, I think we're done. Now you can run off to who knows where."

"Didn't I tell you?" She waggled her eyebrows. "I'm staying in Henryetta."

My breath froze in my chest. "For how long?"

She grinned, but I could see the hint of challenge in her eyes. "As long as it takes."

I spun around and left the restaurant, afraid to ask what she meant by that. Besides, she wouldn't have told me anyway.

As I climbed into my car, I saw Kate emerge from Merilee's with a look of determination on her face. When she didn't head to her car, I got nervous. What was she up to? She took a long look at Rose's office, and my heart leapt into my throat. She knew so much about everything else, did she already know about RBW Landscaping? Maybe the attention I'd given it earlier had tipped her off. But Rose's truck was gone, and Kate turned around and headed toward the courthouse. Was her source of information in the courthouse? Could it be Mason Deveraux?

No doubt about it, I had some sleuthing of my own to do now.

And the most important thing was for me to find out Kate's real end game.

Chapter Nine
Hilary

Henryetta, Arkansas.

Of all the places that man could pick to live, he chose Henryetta in Fenton County. I hated this God-forsaken cesspool of a town. But then he probably counted on that when he chose to move here, thinking I wouldn't follow him.

But he was wrong. I would follow him anywhere.

Following him was yet another way of proving how much I loved him, although I'd never given him reason to doubt me. I'd proved my love for him over and over and over again, even when other women paraded through his life.

I was used to philandering. My own father was guilty of it. J.R. Simmons was the king of it. Most successful political men were promiscuous. I'd accepted this from an early age. My duty was to support Joe in his political role. Only Joe wasn't stepping up to fulfill his duty, and I was catching the brunt of both of our families' disappointment.

My father and J.R. had been friends since grade school, even attending college together. Both families came from oil money, but the Simmons family had evolved into law and then politics. J.R.'s father was a U.S. Representative, and he expected similar greatness from his son. But J.R.'s strength lay in reading people within minutes of meeting them, a talent he used to detect a person's strengths and weaknesses and exploit them to meet his own ends. This would have been a superlative attribute in a politician, of course, but as a politician, J.R. Simmons would have been a puppet. He was much more effective as the puppet master. He ran multiple businesses, broadening his influence through forming connections with all the people in high places around him.

J.R. had many men in his pocket, but what he really wanted was a man he could truly own. A man who would do whatever he wanted, whenever he wanted, without question. He needed a son.

And as soon as his wife was pregnant with that son, he started to plan for the boy's future. In exchange for Ed Wilder's help in propelling J.R.'s soon-to-be-born son into the White House, J.R.'s son would marry Ed's soon-to-be-born daughter. A simple handshake, several pats on the back, a couple of whiskey chasers, and my fate was sealed. Before either of us were even born. They never once questioned that they had agreed to an arranged marriage, something unheard of in the twentieth century. It never occurred to them that their children might rebel.

And I hadn't. I'd understood my role from the beginning, since before I could read or write. One day, come what may, I would marry Joseph Simmons.

Only Joe *never* knew. His father felt it best to keep the news from him until he was older. After all, young Joe needed to focus on preparing for his future political career. Camps and debate. Current events and diplomacy. Joe learned at his grandfather's knee. Literally. J.R.'s most cherished photo was taken in his father's Washington, D.C., office—it showed a toddling Joe next to his formidable grandfather in a wooden chair, with J.R. behind them, looking down on the two most important men in his life.

The photo was more accurate than anyone could guess.

But by the end of Bill Simmons' political career, his savvy young son was calling the shots, all while grooming his son to take his father's place.

J.R. had a master plan. His father would stay in the House until Joe graduated from law school, then Joe would take over Bill's seat in the next election. And everything was going according to plan until Bill had the audacity to have a heart attack when Joe was in fifth grade.

Kate was right about one thing. The three of us had grown up together. We'd shared an idyllic childhood. Summers spent at the Simmons house and playing in their pool. Family dinners and combined trips. I was with Joe and Kate Simmons more than with any of my other friends, and our parents loved it, always watching Joe and me with a special look.

But even though we spent all that time together, I never saw Joe as a brother. Of course, my mother's whispers helped with that, but I was certain Joe had never viewed me as a sibling either. We had always been close, but it was in fifth grade, the year Bill Simmons died, that our relationship changed.

Our parents had enrolled us in Cotillion, and the class covered meal etiquette. Joe and I giggled over the fact that so many of our fellow attendees couldn't tell the difference between a salad and a dessert fork.

Joe's mother Betsy picked us up after our class, and she watched us with a smile as we tumbled into the back of her Cadillac. "How'd it go?" she asked.

"It's a total waste of time," Joe grumbled. "Hilary and I know everything already. We could teach the class. Do we have to go next week?"

"Yes." Betsy turned around and started to drive out of the parking lot. "Next week you start dance lessons."

"*Dance* lessons," Joe grumbled. "What on earth do I need to learn dance for? I don't have to wear tap or ballet shoes do I?"

"No, Joseph," she murmured good-naturedly. "You won't be learning tap dancing or even ballet—although your grandmother and I will teach you how to appreciate attending a ballet soon enough. But in Cotillion you will learn to waltz and do the foxtrot."

"Is that anything like fox hunting? Dad said he'd take me hunting for quail next month."

"No," she chuckled. "Although I suspect you'll have more fun quail hunting than you will learning the foxtrot. But Hilary will be there with you, so that will help to make it more fun."

Joe turned to me and smiled.

My heart warmed in my chest and my breath caught. While I'd always known we would get married one day, *that* was the moment I fell in love with Joe Simmons.

But he still only saw us as friends. My mother hushed my fears before I went to bed that night. "Don't worry, Hilary," she said, smoothing back my hair. "Joe's young. Much too young to fall in love."

"He doesn't even know he's supposed to marry me," I said, big fat tears falling down my cheeks. "He's been playing foursquare with Margery Pope at recess. I think he likes *her*."

My mother's fingers delicately lifted my chin until my gaze met hers. "Hilary, I wish I could tell you that your life with Joe Simmons will be an easy one, but if he's anything like his father, I'm sure it won't be. But you must have faith that everything will work out in the end."

That was enough to calm me for the moment. For if Joe was going to be like his daddy, I wasn't sure I wanted to marry him after all.

Even at the tender age of ten, I knew J.R. Simmons was capable of terrible things. The J.R. I usually saw was all campaign smiles and cheerfulness, but I had seen something the summer before.

I was at the Simmons' house swimming with Kate and Joe that day. Kate and I had a disagreement over something stupid, so I stomped inside. Only I forgot my towel and I immediately began to shiver in the air-conditioned house. Rather than go back outside, I decided to head up to the laundry room and see if I could find a towel there. As I walked past J.R.'s office, I heard strange sounds. I hurried down the hall, partially out of my fear and partially because my teeth were chattering. I was excited to find a load of towels tumbling in the dryer, with only a few minutes left on the cycle. I opened the door, pulled out a fluffy towel, and wrapped it around my shoulders, letting the warmth seep into my body. By the time I walked back down the hall, I had forgotten about the strange noises until I reached the office door. I pressed my ear against the wood, trying to figure out what was happening. My eyes flew wide when I realized a woman was crying inside. Worried she was hurt, I broke a cardinal rule of the Simmons household: *Never* go into J.R. Simmons' office without an invitation. Truth be told, Joe, Kate and I had broken the rule over a half dozen times without anything bad happening, but I was still cautious as I slowly turned the knob and cracked the door, pressing my cheek to the doorframe to see inside.

My heart thudded wildly and fear raced through my body as I registered the sight of a woman bent over the side of J.R.'s desk—her torso pressed flat to the surface, her hands splayed out beside her head, and her face turned to face the back wall. Her green floral skirt was pushed up to her waist so I could see her pale, round butt cheeks. J.R. stood behind her, his pants dropped to his knees. One hand was pressed hard on her back, keeping her down as she struggled against him. But his front pounded against her with a violence I had never seen before. There was a look of pure evil in his eyes, but his smile was what scared me the most. I was too young to understand what I was seeing other than that J.R. Simmons, the man who'd been like a second father to me, was purposely hurting the woman on the desk.

He gave several last hard shoves against her, making her cry out again, and he let out a loud groan before grabbing a handful of her short blonde hair and lifting her head slightly off the desk. "Is that what you had in mind when you offered to repay me for your husband's transgressions, Della?"

She didn't answer, only whimpered softly.

He released her hair and her face fell onto the desk. His hands palmed her ass and a wider grin spread across his face. "Yes, I do believe we *can* work something out."

I gasped. He was going to hurt her again.

I shut the door as quickly and quietly as I could, but it wasn't fast enough. J.R.'s face turned toward the door as I closed it, and I couldn't be sure if he'd seen me or not. I ran down the hall and into the kitchen, unable to face Joe and Kate but unsure of where else to go. I opened the pantry door and huddled in the back for several minutes before the door started to open. Terrified that J.R. had found me and would hurt me too, my eyes burned with tears. Momma had told me strong Southern women do not cry in public, so I swallowed them down.

But it was Roberta's warm mocha-colored face that filled the doorway. She took one look at me and knew something was up. "What on earth are you doin' in here, girl?"

I jumped to my feet and ran to her, wrapping my arms around her wide waist and burying my face into her breast.

Within less than a second I was cocooned in her arms. "Baby girl, you're shakin' like a leaf. What's got you so scared?"

I shook my head against her, fighting back tears again. "Don't tell him. Please don't tell him."

"Who you talkin' about?" she asked, but even as the words escaped, a certain knowing crept in at the end. She grabbed my arms and pulled me away from her, trying to mask the fear in her eyes. "Tell him what?"

I never considered the possibility that she might not know whom I was talking about. Only one man could induce such fear. "That I saw," I whispered.

She took a step back, her hands shaking, but then she bent to look into my face. "Saw what, baby girl?"

I squeezed my eyes shut and violently shook my head. I couldn't repeat it. I wouldn't.

"Did you look into Mr. J.R.'s office?"

I nodded, my chin quivering, and the tears finally began to fall.

She pulled me back to her chest, rubbing my back in sweeping circles. "Ain't nobody tellin' nobody nothin', ya hear?" She squeezed me tight to her and her heart raced in my ear. "Nobody's tellin' nothin'."

"Okay."

"Roberta." J.R.'s voice boomed in the kitchen.

Roberta's eyes flew open wide and she glanced over her shoulder, then back down at me. "You act normal. You understand?" She spoke in a whisper, but her tone was stern and absolute.

"Yes, ma'am," I whispered back, wiping away my tears.

"In here, Mr. J.R.," Roberta said in a cheery voice. "Miss Hilary is helping me make cookies." She grabbed a container of flour and shoved it at me before grabbing sugar and chocolate chips.

I reluctantly followed her out of the pantry, leaving my damp towel on the floor where it had fallen when Roberta hugged me. I started to avert my eyes from J.R., but then I remembered hearing Daddy tell someone that he always knew when the people in his courtroom were guilty because they couldn't look him in the eye. So I lifted my gaze to his and forced a smile. "Hello, Mr. J.R. I didn't know you were home from work already."

I set the flour on the island, trying not to shiver from the cold.

"Why aren't you out swimming with Joe and Kate?" he asked, an edge of suspicion in his voice.

"Oh, you know those kids," Roberta grumbled. "They always spattin' about somethin'. Kate hurt Hilary's feelings, so I told her to come in here and help me make some cookies."

He watched us both carefully, then turned his gaze to me. "Hilary, were you outside my office door just now?" His voice was sweet, but I didn't trust him for a second.

I shook my head slowly. "No, sir."

"She's been in here with me for a good ten to fifteen minutes," Roberta said, pulling out a mixing bowl. "Why you askin'?"

He looked over his shoulder, suddenly unsure. "Never mind." Then he walked out of the room, leaving us behind.

Roberta carried on with the cookies for a few minutes before she looked down at me, terror in her eyes. "I don't know what you saw in that man's office, but you can never tell a soul any of it, you hear?"

I nodded, tears filling my eyes again.

She licked her lips, then leaned down until our faces were only inches apart. "Evil goes on in that office, baby girl, so you best stay far, far away."

"Yes, ma'am."

She wrapped an arm around my shoulders and snugged me into a side hug. "That's my good girl."

Chapter Ten
Hilary

I heeded Roberta's advice and stayed far away from J.R.'s office after that day. I also never told anyone about what I'd seen. In the beginning I felt guilty that I hadn't done anything to help that poor woman. But as I grew older, I realized two things: one, it would have been pointless because no one, even the police, crossed J.R. Simmons, and two, J.R. would have made my life utterly miserable. And I told myself that Della's husband must have done something terribly wrong for J.R. to hurt her like that as payment. She had to have known that going to him would be painful.

And as the years went by, Joe and I began to date on and off. He would often leave me for breaks with other girls—a behavior that displeased my parents, but made Joe's parents even more unhappy.

When I was seventeen, Joe had broken up with me for the fourth time and was dating some white trailer trash girl who was known for her epic drinking and whoring. I was at home eating dinner with my parents one Friday night. In the middle of the meal, my father let me know how disappointed he and my mother were with my failure to keep Joe in line.

"I'm doing my best," I said in a huff, once again wondering how I'd gotten stuck in this mess. I loved Joe, I truly did, but why would I want to be with a man who always seemed to want someone else? Yet when I mentioned that fact to my parents, my mother leaned over the corner of the dining room table and slapped my face.

I clutched my stinging cheek, fighting back tears as she pointed her finger at me. "You have no idea what's at stake, Hilary. Your father's future is riding on this."

"No one asked me if I wanted to marry Joe Simmons!" But despite my protests, I would have done anything for him to say he loved me. I would have sold my soul to get him to propose.

"J.R. wants to see you," my father said in a brusque voice.

My body froze in panic. "Why?" I forced out.

"He and Betsy want to talk to you about Joe."

At least Betsy would be there too. Some of the tension left my body. "When?"

"Eight o'clock."

I glanced at the clock on the wall. It was already 7:30.

My mother put her napkin on the table. "Why don't you go upstairs and freshen up and put on a pretty dress before you leave? You can wear the peach one I bought you last week."

My hands began to shake. "Why? I've never dressed up just to talk to Betsy and J.R."

My mother's eyes narrowed. "Maybe that's the problem, Hilary. You're not putting enough effort into your appearance. If you were…."

The unspoken implication was clearly understood by everyone. If I had put in more effort, period, none of us would be in this situation.

I stood, clenching my fists at my side. "I don't want to go. Someone else can marry Joe Simmons." It ripped my heart out to say it, but I couldn't handle the pressure all four of them were putting on me. It had only gotten worse now that we were in the second semester of our junior year.

My father's fist banged on the table. "You will go to the Simmons house even if I have to drive you there myself and drop you off at the door. Do you understand?"

My tears broke loose. "Daddy."

His eyes softened. "You have to go, Hilary. No one tells J.R. no. You should know that by now."

I did. All too well. I went upstairs and brushed my hair and put on the conservative peach-colored dress, then headed downstairs. My mother was in the kitchen, looking over her shoulder so she could catch me before I left. She hurried over to me, cringing when she glanced at my face and saw the fading marks from her hand.

"Hilary, my darling. You are so much like me." She offered me a soft smile. "I've always told you that Joe Simmons is your future, but your father and I think that tonight J.R. is planning to break the deal he made with your father."

Cold dread crept up my back. "What does that mean?"

"It means if you don't give him the answers he wants, your father will probably lose his seat on the bench. And he can kiss his Arkansas Supreme Court nomination goodbye."

I studied her face in wonderment—too stunned to feel anger. Seventeen years ago, J.R. had made an arrangement with a man who was nearly his equal. It was obvious the balance of power had shifted more than I'd anticipated. But even more shocking was the fact that my parents had placed my father's entire career on the ability of their teenage daughter to snag a boy.

This couldn't be happening.

As I drove to the Simmons house, I found myself hoping Kate was home. We were nearly mortal enemies by that point, so no one would be more shocked by that hope than Kate. But I knew I'd feel safer if she were in the house.

I pulled my BMW into the circular drive and parked, taking deep breaths before I could make myself get out of the car. I was being silly. Why was I so nervous? Would it really be the end of the world if the Simmonses decided I wasn't worthy enough to continue my pursuit of their son? No, it would be a huge relief. They could yell, but they would never strike me. And if my father lost his spot on the bench? Well, it would be his fault, not mine.

I knocked on the front door, expecting Betsy to answer since it was so late in the evening, but to my surprise, it was Gerald, the Simmonses' butler.

"Good evening, Miss Hilary," he said as he opened the door wider.

I crossed the threshold, overcome with the feeling that something was really off. I took a deep breath and told myself I was being silly. Yet when Gerald didn't ask to take my light coat, my gut instinct was confirmed.

"Follow me, please."

I almost bolted, but where would I go? My father would follow through with his earlier threat and bring me back. No one in town would help me if I decided to buck my parents' and the Simmonses' plan for me, and I had no money. The reality was that I was stuck. I reassured myself with the thought that I only needed to see this night through…then I could go home and come up with a plan.

Gerald stopped in front of J.R.'s office door, knocking before he pushed it open. "Mr. Simmons, Miss Hilary has arrived."

"Thank you, Gerald." J.R. sat behind his desk, a cigar in one hand, a crystal tumbler in the other. "Hilary, come in." There was no sign of Betsy in the room.

I reluctantly stepped inside, surprised when I heard the door close behind me and the lock click into place.

Cold sweat broke out on my neck, but I kept my back ramrod stiff. My mother had pounded the art of never showing your true feelings into me. I only hoped I could maintain the ruse.

He watched me, an amused grin forming on his face when I stayed close to the door. I knew him well enough to know he liked to watch people squirm. I decided the best course of action would be to pretend like the meeting was no big deal. I reached for the belt of my coat and started to unknot it.

"Leave it on," he said, his voice gruff.

My hand froze, and I looked up at him in shock. Why would he want me to leave my coat on? Maybe this meeting would be blessedly short.

But I'd given him exactly the reaction he'd wanted. He'd gained the upper hand. He stubbed out the cigar in a glass tray on his desk, then took a long sip of his drink before setting down the tumbler. "Stay where you are."

"Why?" I asked before I could stop myself.

"Because I'm J.R. Simmons, Hilary. I can do whatever the hell I want, and even better, I can *make* people do whatever the hell I want." He paused and stared into my eyes, an evil smile tipping up the corners of his lips. "You of all people should know that."

My stomach dropped to my feet, promptly followed by the blood rushing from my head. *He knows I saw him that day.* Panic rose up in my chest, but I pushed it down. Panicking would do me no good. I needed to keep calm and reason myself out of this. I wasn't sure what *this* was, but I knew it couldn't be good.

"You want to have this discussion while I'm wearing my coat. Fine." I stood with one hand at my side, making sure my fingers hung loose and looked relaxed. My purse was cradled in the crook of my other arm and I was trying my best to portray the unaffected, aloof Southern woman, just like my mother had taught me.

J.R. seemed amused. "Do you know why you're here?"

"My father said you and Betsy wanted to talk to me." I cast a quick glance at the office door before returning my gaze to him.

"Betsy has gone to Little Rock for a shopping weekend and won't be home until Sunday evening. Kate is sleeping over at a friend's house. I told Gerald to take off for the evening after you arrived. And Joe?" He paused and picked up his drink, staring into the glass before looking up at me. "We both know Joe's busy screwing a whore."

My cheeks flushed in embarrassment.

"Do you know why Joe is screwing a whore, Hilary?"

"Because he's like his father and will chase any piece of ass?" I asked, then swallowed the gasp that rose in my throat. *Good God.* What had possessed me to say that?

J.R. stood, his face expressionless as he walked around the edge of his desk. "Betsy thinks we should cut you loose. That you're not enough to hold our young Joe in line. And I was about to agree with her, but first I wanted to see if you have any backbone." He grinned. "And there it is, kept carefully hidden under your genteel exterior." He began to walk around me in a wide circle. "Joe is more headstrong than I'd hoped he would be. It's going to take a strong woman to live up to the task of keeping him in line."

I kept perfectly still, wondering what he was getting at and why I still had my coat on.

"Your parents have done a wonderful job of teaching you how to be a politician's wife, but almost to the point of driving all the fire out of you. My goal tonight is to see if we can fan those embers to life."

I swallowed. "What does that mean?'

He stopped circling me and stood at my side. "Do you know why Joe is fucking that girl tonight?"

"Because he's a teenage boy and he can't keep his dick in his pants?"

I expected him to hit me, but he laughed instead. "That's true. But the real question is why isn't he with you?"

Oh, God.

"Are you a virgin, Hilary?"

"That is none of your business."

"It *is* my business. If you are going to marry my son one day, your sexual history is very much my business."

I could refuse to answer, but he'd weasel the answer out of me one way or another. Besides, I had nothing to be ashamed of. "Yes, I'm a virgin."

"Has Joe ever tried to screw you?"

I cringed at his crassness. "You should ask Joe that question."

"Joe's not here, and I'm asking you."

"No."

"Why not?"

I took a breath, trying to keep from shaking. I wanted to run from the room, but I knew the door was locked and it couldn't be opened without a key. I wanted to say because Joe was a gentleman who had never treated me with anything other than respect. But the fact that he was currently screwing Kelly Rogers belied that concept.

"How far have you and Joe gone, Hilary?" He reached over and trailed his hand down my cheek and down my neck, stopping at the hollow of my throat.

My breath came in heavy pants. This wasn't happening. This wasn't happening.

His grin turned wicked. "Does that turn you on?"

"What? No!" I took a step backward, but J.R. stepped in front of me and gripped my wrist.

"Today it occurred to me that you don't know how to make my son happy."

"It's not my job to make Joe happy."

J.R.'s free hand reached up for my neck, placing enough pressure on my windpipe to make me uncomfortable. "Oh, but it *is*." He slowly removed his hand

and took several steps back. "I'm going to give you a very special gift, Hilary. I'm going to teach you the art of seducing a man."

I slowly shook my head.

"When I'm done with you, you could work as a high-class escort…which you might end up doing if you continue to fail with Joe."

"I'm not sleeping with you."

He sat on the edge of his desk. "Not to worry. There won't be any sleeping involved."

"I'm a minor. You can't have sex with a minor."

"I thought we'd already established that I can do whatever I want."

"No. I won't do it." I turned around and reached for the doorknob, confirming it was locked. I pounded on the door, screaming and begging for someone to help. I expected J.R. to try and stop me, but he merely sipped his drink and waited.

When I quieted, he said, "You are not leaving this room until I am satisfied that you have properly learned your lesson. We'll begin when you're ready."

I wanted to break out into hysterical tears, but he'd love that and I would give this man no more than what I absolutely *had* to give. I took a deep breath, wiped my tears, then turned to face him.

"Move to the center of the room."

I set my purse on the floor by the door, then did as he'd ordered.

"The art of seduction is catching the man's attention. Now take off your coat." I started to unknot my belt, but he stopped me. "No. Slowly unknot it, then take your time unbuttoning."

I did it, staring into his amused eyes as I tried to swallow the bile in my throat. I hated this man more than I'd ever hated anyone in my life, but there wasn't a damn thing I could do about it. Once my coat hung open, I waited for his next instruction.

His mouth quirked to one side in a cocky grin. "Yes, you should look the man you're seducing in the eyes, and given the circumstances, I'll forgive the defiance. Now slowly slip the coat down your arms and let it fall to the floor."

I did as he'd instructed, then waited. If he wanted a striptease with this dress, he was going to be disappointed. It zipped down the back.

"Come here."

Every fiber of my being told me to disobey, but what would be the point? It took five steps to reach him, five torturous steps. And when I stopped, his hands settled on my hips and he pulled my pelvis firm against his erection. I swallowed my nausea. I wasn't sure I could do this. I *couldn't* do this.

"*No.*" I jerked backward, but his hands held me in place.

He leaned back slightly and studied my face, his own empty of any emotion. "No?" Then he spun me around in his grasp. One hand stayed on my stomach, keeping me in front of him, while the other stroked my ass. "You were the one who watched me that day. How much did you see?"

"I don't know," I mumbled, fear making my tongue heavy. I fought the tears burning in my eyes. I couldn't lose control. Not with this man. I might not survive the experience.

"You don't know," he chuckled as his front hand rose to my breast. "Do you remember what she looked like, pinned flat to my desk as I pounded her from behind? Do you remember her whimpers and cries? *Do you?*"

My eyes squeezed shut and a traitorous tear slid down my cheek. How could this be happening? "Yes."

His hands painfully squeezed my flesh and his voice took on a menacing tone I'd never heard before. "I can fuck you that way if you don't cooperate, or I can show you how to make a man so happy he'll never consider leaving your bed. Which would you prefer, Hilary? The painful way—which can be fun too—or the pleasurable way? It's your choice, my dear."

It was no choice at all, and he knew it. I was tempted to tell him to screw me from behind and get it over with, but I knew it wouldn't be that easy. "I'll cooperate."

"Wise choice for your first time." His hand slid down my stomach and my leg, then lifted the hem of my dress. "But you'll do much more than *cooperate*."

I learned many things that night.

The art of giving a blowjob.

The fact that J.R. Simmons clearly took Viagra.

That sex was power.

My tears only got him off more.

It was to be the first of several months of weekly "lessons," but I didn't know that yet.

When he was finally done with my lesson that night, he told me I was free to go. He sat in his leather chair, wearing his boxers and his open dress shirt, sipping the drink he'd made me refresh for him. I picked up my clothes and quickly dressed, making him chuckle as I fumbled with the zipper. I left it gaping open and put on my coat, then bolted for the door, only then remembering it was locked.

"Don't make plans next Friday," he murmured as he rose from his chair. I heard the desk drawer open and close, and I hoped to God he'd retrieved the key. He walked up behind me, only stopping when his chest was pressed to my back. My gasp only earned laughter. "You were a very good student, Hilary. And not to worry, soon you'll love it when I touch you."

That day would never come, but I kept that thought to myself in case he decided to start that lesson tonight. His hand slowly slipped into my coat pocket. "Go see the doctor on that paper and start taking birth control pills."

I gasped, realizing we'd had unprotected sex.

"And get some sexy lingerie. Wear black lace next Friday." He leaned down and kissed my neck. "And let your father know his position is safe. For now."

Had my father known this would happen? *Please, God, don't let that be true.* "How many…?" I couldn't finish the question.

"I'll continue to screw you until Joe *does.*"

He unlocked the door and I stumbled out of the office, feeling numb, sick to my stomach, and deeply ashamed. The door shut behind me, and I was startled to see Roberta in the hallway, emerging from the kitchen.

"Hilary?" she asked in surprise.

I shook my head in embarrassment, fighting tears as I ran for the front door. Would Roberta think I'd deserved my fate, just as I'd thought poor Della did? I couldn't look her in the eyes and see her disappointment and condemnation. Not from her.

I climbed into my car as she ran out the door.

"Hilary!" she shouted as I pulled around the circular drive and out of the gate.

I sped home, going twenty miles over the speed limit. I wanted a police officer to pull me over so when he asked why I was speeding I could tell him that J.R. Simmons had just raped me. But it wasn't rape, as J.R. had pointed out while I lay on my back, without any fight, spreading my legs for him to screw me. Several times.

No, I'd just become his whore.

My mother was waiting for me when I got home, an anxious look on her face. For a brief moment, I thought maybe she suspected what had happened in J.R.'s office, but she seemed more concerned about whether their deal had been broken. "Don't worry, Mother," I said as I climbed the stairs with achy legs. "You and Dad are safe."

"So you worked it out with J.R."

I slowly spun around to face her. "J.R. made me give him a blowjob and took my virginity on his desk, all in the name of keeping Joe happy in the bedroom. Does that sound like working it out to you?"

I wasn't sure what I expected from her. That she'd accuse me of lying? Get angry and call the police? I got neither reaction.

She lifted her chin, her jaw clenching. "Whatever it takes."

My mouth dropped. "You would whore your daughter out to get what you want?"

"It's time to grow up, Hilary. The world revolves around sex. How do you think I got your dad? J.R. is doing you a favor. Joe has a wandering eye, just like his father and grandfather before him. If you can make him happy in bed, you have a better chance of keeping him there. And if anyone would know what keeps a man happy, it's J.R. Simmons."

"I'm seventeen years old!"

She shrugged, her eyes hard. "And you're a year younger than I was when I started to have sex to get what I wanted." She climbed two steps. "Sex is a powerful weapon, Hilary. It's brought many a man to his knees. The better you are at it, the more control you'll have over your relationship with Joe." She paused. "And J.R. is very, very good."

My mother had screwed J.R. Simmons. How perverted were these people? "I will never be like that," I said in a tight, shaky voice. "I will *never* manipulate Joe with sex."

"There are far worse things, Hilary." She sighed. "You've had a busy day. Go to bed and get a good night's sleep."

She'd equated getting raped multiple times by her best friend's husband to *a busy day*.

I spun around and ran into my room, locking the door behind me. The rest of the night was spent trying to formulate an escape plan. I couldn't live through another night in J.R.'s office. If I stole my mother's jewelry and ran off to Little Rock, I could sell it at a pawn shop and live on the cash until I found a job. But Little Rock was too close. They'd find me there. Maybe I could go to Memphis. Or Tulsa. But I couldn't leave now. I would need more of a head start. I would run away on Monday morning. My mother would think I'd left for school, which would buy me a good eight hours to get far, far away from them.

Even with my flimsy plan in place, I barely slept, and the next day I refused to open my door when my mother knocked. Well into the afternoon, I heard another knock and shouted, "Go away!"

"Hilary, it's Joe."

My pulse pounded in my head. Did he know? Did he know the disgusting things his father had made me do? I couldn't face him, but I knew him well enough to know he wouldn't go away until he saw me. I slid off my bed and padded to the door, opening it a crack. "What do you want?"

"Can I come in? Your mom called and told me you weren't feeling well."

"And you came over?"

"Of course," he said in disbelief. "I care about you."

But not enough. If only he'd loved me enough, I wouldn't have been forced to deal with the humiliation I'd endured the night before. Part of me wanted to slam the door in his face and tell him to leave me alone forever, but I couldn't. I still loved the boy standing in my doorway, and it only made me hate myself more. I opened the door the rest of the way and let him in.

He stared at my rumpled bed covered in wadded tissues. "Do you have a cold? Is that why your nose is all red and your eyes are puffy?"

I wanted to laugh. I wanted to cry. Instead, I nodded. "Yeah. It's a cold."

He hesitated, as if he could tell something between us had changed. "When my dad found out you weren't feeling well, he asked me to bring you something."

"What is it?" I asked suspiciously as I sat on my bed, fear warming my blood.

Joe sat next to me and pulled an envelope out of his pocket. "I don't know. He said for you to read it while I'm here so I can bring back a response."

I reached a shaky hand toward him, but instead of handing the envelope to me, he set it in his lap and caught my hand between both of his.

"Hey, are you okay?" He sounded worried. "You're shaking and your hands are freezing."

"I'm fine. Low blood sugar. I haven't eaten today."

"Let me get you something. Whatever you want."

"I only want you," I whispered, fighting back tears.

He gave me a cocky grin. "You've already got me, Hils." But when he noticed how upset I was, he sat back on the bed and gave me a soft kiss. "How about we spend the whole day together? I'll go get a pizza and rent a cheesy movie and we'll hole up here. Sound good?"

I started to cry. I felt dirty even though I must have showered five times since coming home the night before. J.R. Simmons claimed he was teaching me how to keep Joe, but now I felt as if I didn't deserve him.

His hand cupped my cheek and he kissed me, a deep soulful kiss for a boy of seventeen. "I know it hurts you when I go out with other girls, but don't you feel trapped by our parents' expectations?"

I cried even harder.

"Hils, I love you. I do. But when we're finally together, I want to be with *you* and no one else. Does that makes sense? Which means I want to date all the girls I'd never bring home to my parents while we're too young for it to matter."

I wrapped my arms around his neck, still sobbing. He had no idea how much it *did* matter.

"Hey." His voice took on a hard tone. "Something happened. You're not one of those weeping girls, so something bad must have happened."

I took a deep breath. If I told him, would he believe me? Would he help me? The look in his eyes told me he would. Maybe he'd run away with me. He hated the weight of his parents' expectations as much as I hated the expectations everyone had for me. Maybe it was time for me to come clean and tell him everything.

Understanding lit up his sad eyes. "Oh. I'm so stupid. You heard about Roberta. I know you loved her too."

My blood turned to ice. "What about Roberta?"

"She's gone. Quit. She left El Dorado without even saying goodbye."

I shook my head in dismay. "*What?*"

"Dad said she quit last night. The weird thing is she wasn't even working last night. Kate is devastated, and so am I. She's—she *was* more of a mom than Betsy ever was, which is what makes this so hard." His voice wavered. "I never thought she'd just leave me."

Could her sudden resignation have something to do with me? "I didn't know…"

He took my hand and squeezed. "I'm going to get our pizza and a movie. When I come back, you can tell me what's bothering you." He absently picked up the envelope in his lap and started for the door.

I watched the envelope, terrified of its contents. "Hey, Joe. Did you say you had something for me?"

"Oh…yeah." He handed it to me. "I almost forgot."

He gave me a lingering kiss, then walked out the door. I waited to rip it open until I heard the front door downstairs open and close.

Hilary,

I'm sure you've heard the sad news about Roberta. While I've told Kate and Joe that Roberta resigned and left without even telling them goodbye, the truth is I let her go. You have only yourself to blame. Just like you ran to her nearly eight years ago, you ran to her last night and asked her to come to your aid. And now she's gone.

I need you to keep this entire situation to yourself. If you do not, I will have Roberta arrested for felony theft for stealing from the family who trusted her for years. If you dare breathe a single word to anyone about our arrangement, she will rot away in prison for what's left of her natural life.

Joe is awaiting your answer. And right now I'm thinking of all the delectable things we're going to do to each other at your next lesson. Tell Joe your answer is that you can't wait. I'll ask him specifically what you said, so do be sure to be a good girl and get it right. Think about poor Roberta.

J.R.

I broke into fresh sobs. I hadn't asked Roberta to intervene on my behalf, but she must have put two and two together. Now her life hinged on my actions. Screw J.R. and save her, or run away and have her put in prison for the rest of her life. She was in her sixties. She'd never survive there. J.R. knew I loved her too much to let that happen.

But J.R.'s promise…*threat*…echoed in my head. *I'll continue to screw you until Joe does.* His ultimate goal was for me to have sex with Joe and keep him as mine. One way or another, I was going to have sex, whether I wanted to or not. If I had to pick between the two men, it wasn't even a matter of choosing.

I knew I could convince Joe to have sex with me. And I was right. As we lay on my bed that night, watching a stupid rom-com, I seduced my future husband. It was even easier than I'd expected. I employed a few tricks I'd learned courtesy of Joe's father, feeling dirtier and dirtier by the minute, but I justified my actions by reminding myself that I had no choice. This was the destiny that had been planned for me, and my seduction of Joe would make both of our lives easier. Even though I could barely look at myself in the mirror for weeks afterward.

But if I'd thought that sleeping with Joe would end my seduction lessons with J.R., I was devastatingly wrong.

My life lessons with J.R. Simmons had only just begun.

And now I was in Henryetta, Arkansas, twelve years later, still trying to make Joe Simmons mine.

Just like everyone else in my life, Rose Gardner underestimated me. Sure, she might be with Mason Deveraux right now, but Joe couldn't let her go. And as long as Joe couldn't let her go, she was a threat. I hadn't gone to hell and back to give up now. There was too much at stake. I pressed my hand to my still-flat stomach. This baby was supposed to make Joe marry me. I'd never expected him to put up such a fight. Only further proof of how deep Rose Gardner had sunk her claws.

As long as Joe held out hope that Rose would come back to him, he would never marry me. With J.R.'s deadline looming around the corner, I knew I needed to step up my game.

One thing was certain: Rose Gardner needed to go. And it had to be soon.

Chapter Eleven
Mason

I arrived at Merilee's a few minutes before noon. I had planned to walk over to Rose's office, but her truck wasn't out front. Parking around the courthouse and town square was lighter than it was most weekdays, so it wouldn't have been hard to find. She'd gone somewhere. And that made me nervous.

The nature of her business had her traveling all around the county, of course, so that wasn't what made me nervous. It was the whole J.R. Simmons mess that had me on edge. Joe's text had confirmed that my own life was still in danger. It wasn't a huge stretch to think hers might be as well. Only I wasn't sure what to do about that. All the more reason to tell her what I could so she'd be more careful, if that were even possible for her. She seemed to land herself in more dangerous situations than any other person I knew. The fact that she always managed to get out of them was the one reassurance that kept me from insisting on putting her under twenty-four-hour protection.

When I walked in the door, Bonnie, one of the waitresses, greeted me from across the emptier-than-usual restaurant. "Hey, Mr. Deveraux. How many?"

I smiled. Moving to Henryetta had been the hardest transition I'd ever made. It was probably the furthest you could get from Little Rock, but I had grown to appreciate that half the people in the downtown area knew who I was and greeted me by name. "Just two today."

"If you're looking for a more romantic table—" she gave me a sly grin and winked, "—you can sit in that table for two in the back corner." She tilted her head in that direction as she served hot plates to a table of customers.

No one would ever call Merilee's romantic, but it did have its own appeal. Rose and I had eaten lunch here together plenty of times before we started seeing each other. But today I was thankful for the added privacy.

I slipped off my coat and took a seat. Several minutes later the bell on the door jingled and Rose walked in, her cheeks pink and her hair—which was loose today—slightly mussed from the wind. As soon as she spotted me in the corner, a warm loving smile broke loose on her face. I watched her walk toward me and I knew I'd give everything I had for this woman—including my life—as long as she continued looking at me like that.

I stood as she approached and helped her off with her coat, draping it over the back of her chair. But before she could sit, I pulled her into my arms and gave her a lingering kiss. When I lifted my head, surprise flashed in her eyes, quickly replaced with playfulness. "I missed you this morning at breakfast."

I grinned down at her, my chest filling with happiness. "I missed you too, but I hope we can make up for it now." I gave her another quick peck and pulled out her chair, then sat down across from her.

She placed her hands on the table, palms flat, and her playfulness faded. "Mason, about this morning—"

Shaking my head, I reached across the table and took her hand in mine. "Rose, if you're trying to apologize, please don't. I'm the one who needs to be offering up an apology."

"I don't like fightin' with you, Mason. I felt awful until you called."

I tightened my grip on her hand. "I don't like fighting with you either, but we have plenty more fights in our future, I'm sure. If one of us is upset, we need to discuss it rather than let it fester and drive a wedge between us."

"I know you're right, but it still makes me feel terrible."

I leaned closer and gave her a wicked smile. "Think of all the makeup sex we can have."

Bonnie walked up to the table, trying to hide the smirk that told me she'd overheard, and Rose's face flushed.

"I told you this spot was more romantic," Bonnie teased. "I only wish I had some wine to serve with your lunch."

The red hue of Rose's face deepened.

I looked up at the waitress and gave Rose's hand another squeeze. "I'll take a club sandwich and a water. Rose?" I asked, glancing over at her.

She pushed out a breath and looked up at the waitress. "A house salad with ranch dressing on the side and iced tea."

As soon as Bonnie walked away with our order, Rose pulled her hand from mine and whacked my arm. "Mason!"

"I'm sorry." I laughed. "I wouldn't have said it if I'd known she was right there."

Her lips pressed into a pout, but the promise of a grin teased the corners of her mouth. "You owe me, big time."

"Anything you want."

"Anything?" She lifted her eyebrows and her voice took a husky tone.

Her words stole my breath away. Some days I still found it hard to believe she was mine. "You know I'd give you anything, Rose."

"Then tell me what you were doin' in Little Rock."

I stared deep into her hazel eyes for a moment. Once I crossed this line, there would be no going back. But this directly involved her. She had a right to know. "You already suspect."

"You're diggin' up dirt on Joe's father." When I nodded, she pressed on. "And did you find anything?"

I sucked in a deep breath to steady my nerves, suddenly having second thoughts. "Yes and no."

"What's that mean?"

I considered telling her about both leads, but I wasn't sure about Dora Middleton's involvement in the possible extortion scheme. Rose was just coming to terms with her birth mother's existence. I didn't want to tell her that Dora might have been involved in criminal activity without more evidence. "It means I found a potential lead that might help us."

She leaned closer and lowered her voice. "What is it?"

I leaned closer as well. "I think I found an incident in Columbia County a year and a half ago. It sounds like a construction company might have bribed county officials to win a bid for an addition to a county government office building."

She shook her head slightly. "What does that have to do with J.R.?"

"He owns the corporation that owns the construction company."

Realization lit up her face, followed fast by skepticism. "Would he really be that sloppy?"

"No. That's part of the problem. All I have so far are rumors. I need to do some digging in Magnolia."

Fear flickered in her eyes. "Is that smart, Mason? Isn't it going to look suspicious if you're digging around in another county?"

"I don't trust anyone else to do this, Rose. They could either botch it up or run to J.R. with the whole story."

"Bribery charges… I know that's bad, but is it really enough to bring him down?"

"Honestly, I don't know. I think it's only the tip of the iceberg, but I won't know until I keep digging."

"Is it really worth the risk? If you go after him and it's not enough…"

"Rose." I waited until she looked me in the eyes. "Don't worry. I intend to be smart about this."

I considered telling her about J.R.'s possible involvement in Fenton County and his request to Joe to let Mick Gentry kill Skeeter Malcolm, but the information had come directly from Joe. I'd given Joe my word not to let Rose know of his involvement in my special project, and she'd want to know where I'd come by the information. I could lie and tell her I'd heard a rumor while I was in Little Rock, but I didn't want to do that. I'd rather lie by omission than tell her a flat-out untruth. And besides, when you came right down to it, it was really an official county matter. Which meant that I couldn't tell her at all.

She was silent for several moments and Bonnie came back with our food. After making sure we had everything we needed, she disappeared back into the kitchen.

Rose picked up her fork and scooped some of her dressing onto her salad. "Did you find out anything else?"

I opened my mouth, suddenly unsure with my choice, but I pressed on. "There are a few other things, but I need more information to know if they are anything of importance."

Hurt flickered in her eyes. "You promised."

I sighed. "I'll tell you if you insist. But I think it will be better if you let me wait to tell you. Will you trust me on this one?"

She glanced to the other side of the room and I questioned my decision. Was I being fair? But she turned back to me and looked into my eyes. "I trust you, Mason. But I hope you're not keeping this to yourself because you think I'm not strong enough to handle it."

"Sweetheart, you are one of the strongest people I know. I would never accuse you of being weak."

She gave a quick nod and looked down at her salad.

Bonnie was talking to another waitress as they bussed a table near ours. The other woman shook her head. "I didn't even know Deputy Simmons had a sister."

"She introduced herself as Kate. I have to admit that I saw a resemblance."

"What's she doin' here?"

"I don't know, but their chat didn't look so friendly."

Rose perked up, obviously listening to the women's conversation. So was I.

"The chief deputy didn't look so happy to be there with her. He barely finished his breakfast before stomping off."

"Families." The older woman tsked and shook her head. "You can't live with them; you can't live without them."

Rose stared at the salt shaker on the table. "I knew Joe had a sister named Kate, but he told me that she took off a couple of years ago," she said in an undertone. "I wonder what she's doin' here."

Rose's interest in Joe's sister seemed more than casual. I shrugged and picked up my water. "Maybe she's here for the nursery's grand reopening next week."

"Maybe..." But she didn't sound convinced.

I decided it might be best to change the subject. "Have you got all the details of the grand openings worked out?"

She smiled. "Violet and I spent the morning going over some ideas. There's gonna be an open house at the nursery, and she's going to market Valentine's gifts. She's ordering a bunch of miniature rose bushes and plans to tell the husbands that they're roses that will last longer than a few days. It's Henryetta, so she's pushing the frugal aspect."

I nodded. "It's actually a good idea."

"Violet was never short on ideas. The problem was that she didn't have enough money to cover them."

"True. So how's she paying for the roses?"

She scowled. "Joe."

I leaned closer, trying to keep my anger in check. I had a feeling this wouldn't be the last time she'd be facing opposition from Violet and Joe. I hated that they put her in this position. "Don't let them railroad you into doing anything you don't want, Rose. You're the majority owner. You can overrule them both."

"I know, but it's a good idea. You said so yourself. I just have to suck up my pride and let it go."

This was Rose's business. I'd vowed to let her run it without my interference, and I'd meant it. But I had a hard time letting it go when I could see they were taking advantage of her generous disposition. "And what about the landscaping business?"

"I think we'll just have a quiet opening. Neely Kate and I are gonna start lining up jobs to work on this spring." She grimaced, then gave me an apologetic smile. "I don't see us bringing in any real income until March or April, but I'm payin' Bruce Wayne and now Neely Kate…I hate to ask…"

I reached across the table and grabbed her hand. "Sweetheart, you don't have to worry. I'll cover the utilities and groceries until you're bringing in money. I don't mind."

Her cheeks flushed and she looked down at her plate. "I'm sorry. I promise I'll pay you back."

"Don't be sorry, and I don't want you to pay me back. If I were out of work, you'd gladly do the same. Hell, you already did that after my condo burned down." I grinned. "At the risk of sounding misogynistic, I like the idea of taking care of you."

She stared into my face. "Thank you."

"I love you, Rose. I said I'd give you anything, and I meant it."

I suspected she had no idea the lengths I'd go to in order to protect her.

Chapter Twelve

Skeeter
One week later

I've worked my ass off for everything I have.

Great-Grandma Idabelle had taught me that anything worth having involved working your ass off. She was one of the few people who'd actually thrived in the Great Depression. Of course, not right away. Prohibition had been alive and in full force in 1930. My great-grandma's husband had deserted her, leaving her with two hungry kids to feed. She filed for divorce—practically unheard of in Fenton County in the 1930s—and decided she'd never feed her kids as a housemaid, not even if she managed to find a good position as a domestic. Only the richest in town kept help in those days. But Grandma had a determination that equaled her well-known temper, and when she settled on her new profession of choice there was no doubt she would succeed.

Her grandfather had been a wildcatter in the late 1800s, so she dug out his recipe and started making moonshine. She faced many a challenge from the Feds, teetotalers from the Methodist church, and the KKK, but Idabelle was no slacker.

The Feds were easy to outmaneuver. She usually got word when a raid was planned. The local men who benefited from her entrepreneurial endeavors would create diversions, giving her ample time to move her stills. But even with the outside help, the Feds managed to catch up to her once, earning her her first arrest. After a handshake deal with the judge, which cost her a crock of her finest spirits, she got off with a hand-slapping fine.

The teetotalers didn't bother her. Grandma Idabelle wasn't one to care for the opinions of gossips and stiffs. If she had been, she would have folded and given up the good fight long before her sorry excuse of a husband left her. The teetotaler women snubbed her in public and tried to get their husbands to refuse her business in town. But their husbands were some of her best customers, buying hooch to drink in their back rooms and barns in their recurrent quest to escape their sharp-tongued wives. Grandma got the last laugh.

The KKK was her biggest problem. In the 1920s they jumped on the Prohibition bandwagon, and although their efforts were focused in the northern part of the state, the local KKK took special notice of Grandma Idabelle. She was a beautiful woman back then, barely twenty years old, and it was her beauty that caught the eye of Burton McHenry, the local KKK leader.

After her husband ran off, Idabelle had vowed never to marry again, but according to rumor, that didn't stop her from seeking out male companionship. Burton McHenry was known to be a harsh man who treated those he considered beneath him poorly, especially African Americans. Great-Grandma was progressive for her time. She hired Coloreds and treated them well, both financially and in terms of respect. What she knew about McHenry's nighttime activities sickened her, as did he. After she told him in no lack of detail what he could do with the appendage in his britches, he vowed to make her pay. Sure enough, several nights later, the KKK showed up on her front lawn.

She sent her terrified children to the cellar, then met her "visitors" on the front porch with a rifle in her hand.

They'd already erected their cross and set it aflame and were marching around in their bedsheets.

"You have no business here, Burton McHenry!" she shouted, holding up her rifle and looking through the sight. "Get the hell off my property!"

"Yer a wicked, wicked woman," he shouted. "Making the men of this town lust after you while you sell your devil spirits and hire darkies."

"I'll hire whoever damn well I please, you yellow-bellied cowards."

"So you're not disputing that you're a temptress?"

Her finger tightened on the trigger. "If the lot of you can't keep your eyes to yourselves, that's yer own damn problem. Have you all set up a cross in Tilly Macon's front yard for making you look at her big tits?"

A couple of the men snickered.

"What you need is a good man to set you straight, Idabelle," the ringleader said. He stood in front of her porch holding a flaming torch in his hand.

"Is this yer way of courtin' me, Burton McHenry?" She lowered the rifle to his crotch. "You got somethin' in there you think I'm dying to get?"

"Don't you threaten me, Idabelle Malcolm." But his voice wavered.

"Why not? Ain't that what yer doin' now? Trying to threaten me into lettin' you screw me?"

A few more men chuckled.

She kept her gun pointed at McHenry's crotch, but looked up at the twenty or so other men in her yard. "Like the lot of you are any better! Yer marching around in yer wives' cast-off sheets like a bunch of boys on All Souls Eve. Do yer wives know what yer doin' out here?" They all fell silent. "Huh? Cat got yer tongue, Darren Porter? How about you, Timothy Hale? Does Maybelle know what yer up to?"

"No ma'am," Hale mumbled.

"If you set my house on fire, I'll come burn every single one of yer houses down too. You all want to spout Bible versus? Well, an eye for an eye is one of my favorites. I'll be happy to show you how much I believe in it."

"Not if yer dead," McHenry growled, pulling a handgun out from the folds of his sheet.

The other men were quick to express their alarm.

"Nobody said nothin' about killin' 'er."

"I'm in charge here," McHenry said, his words drenched with hatred. "I say we're takin' care of this bitch tonight."

"I ain't any part of it," one of the men said, backing up.

"Me neither," another one added, following his friend.

Grandma Idabelle narrowed her eyes. "You might manage to kill me, McHenry, but I guaran-damn-tee you that I'm quicker on the draw and my aim is true. If you pull yer trigger, you'll be walking around without yer dick. Then how are you gonna screw the town?"

The men laughed like the fools they were and McHenry shook with rage. He lowered his gun. "This ain't over, Idabelle."

She kept her gun raised. "It is for me. If I ever see you on my property again, I'll shoot you first and ask questions later." She lowered the gun, but kept it aimed at his private parts. "Now git the hell off my land."

I had begged my great-grandma to tell me that story over and over again when I was a child, along with countless other stories about her exploits. I respected her. Idolized her. I'd never known a woman as strong and courageous as her. She was the model by which I judged every woman, and none had ever come close.

Until I met Rose.

Jed stood beside my desk, glaring at me. "Skeeter, the Hennessey boys are waiting for an answer."

"Hmm?" I asked, shifting in my office chair. I turned my thoughts from Great-Grandma to my right-hand man. "Can you see a reason not to let them have that area?"

"No."

I waved my hand in dismissal. "Then tell them to go for it."

"Why are you so distracted today?" He studied me for a moment. "You're still thinking about stopping by at that reopening, aren't you?"

I shrugged. "I haven't decided yet."

"Skeeter, we both know it's a bad idea." He sat on the edge of the desk. "You need to stay as far away from her in public as possible."

"I'm not gonna talk to her." I chuckled. "I'm just gonna rile up her boyfriend."

"And that's a *really* bad idea. The assistant DA doesn't like you much as it is. I was shocked you saved him from that fire." His gaze penetrated mine. "Why'd you do it?"

I picked up a stapler from my desk and glanced it over. I hadn't told Jed about my new arrangement with Rose, and I hadn't had any contact with her since that night. There were a few things I needed to figure out before I talked to her again.

"You did it for her," Jed said, surprise in his voice.

I slammed down the stapler. "So what if I did? She'd be no good to me if she were moping around all the time, crying about her dead boyfriend. I'll probably need her sooner rather than later. It's important for me to be able to count on her to do her job."

Jed stared at me like he didn't believe my answer. I knew I should correct him. He saw what I'd done—and why I'd done it—as a sign of weakness, which made me a sitting duck. In my world, there was no room for weakness, no room for caring for people. Rose had accused me of sleeping with whores and bimbos, and she was right. I did. I couldn't afford to form personal attachments, not that I'd ever been tempted before. And maybe that's why I strictly dabbled with shallow women. Because the moment I found someone I gave a damn about, that person became fair game. A weapon to be used against me. I should have set Jed straight and told him about the arrangement, but for some reason I couldn't do it. After all, if I couldn't trust Jed, I might as well hang it all up now.

He stood and moved to the back wall, leaning against it. "Why do you think Deveraux called you last week? Do you think he suspects Rose is the Lady in Black?"

I shook my head and kicked my feet up on the desk. "No. If Mr. Mason Deveraux knew, he wouldn't have called me. He would have let me meet my fate with a smile."

"So what's he up to?"

"I don't know. Like I said last week, maybe he came across some intel while playin' undercover DA with Gentry."

Jed hadn't believed that last week, and the sneer on his face made it apparent that his opinion hadn't changed.

"It just doesn't make any sense," Jed muttered, concern wrinkling his forehead. "It would be in Deveraux's favor if you bit the dust, so why would he warn you and offer you immunity to tell him what you know?"

"He obviously knows who's behind the threat. I must be the lesser of the evils."

Jed scoffed. "Not likely."

I shrugged. "Sometimes it's easier to work with the devil you know."

"What if it's Gentry?"

"He seems to be the likely candidate, although it's no secret I've made a few enemies the last few months."

"I've had our trusted guys listening for any hints of what might be going down, but everything's been quiet."

I stared into Jed's face. "Maybe it's not Gentry. Or maybe Gentry's just the tool."

"Then who?"

I kicked my feet off the desk and sat up in my chair. It seemed farfetched to think J.R. Simmons was part of it. Deveraux must have been playing bait and switch. "I think it's almost time to put Lady to work."

"How do you know she'll do it? We took care of the guys who were trying to kill Deveraux."

"She'll do it." I grinned. "Trust me."

The Lady in Black was mine and I intended to use that to my advantage. Soon.

Chapter Thirteen

Rose

My stomach was a bundle of nerves. We'd already had an opening for the nursery, of course, but somehow I was more nervous about this reopening. We had no way of knowing if we'd be welcomed back or shunned now that word had gotten out about Violet's affair. I'd sunk a ton of money into this place, and so had Joe. And even though I hadn't asked him to help me, the responsibility of paying him back was a heavy yoke to carry.

Last time we'd had a big ribbon-cutting ceremony, but this time we were keeping it low-key. We'd put an ad in the paper and spread flyers around town announcing the reopening. There wouldn't be much fanfare—we'd bought a cake from Dena's Bakery, the new bakery in town—and we would be giving five-dollar gift certificates to the first twenty customers. Neely Kate thought using a cake from such a new business was a mistake. We ran the risk of alienating more established businesses, and I needed every supporter I could get. But I decided I would no longer be beholden to this town and its expectations. Which I knew was hypocritical—I wanted them to use our services—but I didn't want to conform their standards. I wanted to have my Dena's Bakery cake and the town's support too.

I hadn't spent much time at the nursery since Joe had made his investment. I usually just dropped by to check on things, but I'd decided to be there on the big day.

Violet was already in the shop when I arrived ten minutes before opening. Neely Kate would be joining us soon to help with the customers, and Joe had said he'd stop by around noon. I was thankful that Joe and I had reached a point where we could be in a room together and be civil. I truly *did* want to be his friend. Mason had given me a silver locket heart that hung from a silver chain for Christmas. Strung on the chain were varied colored stones that represented each of my close friends. The fact that I'd added a stone representing Joe was proof enough that I wanted to be his friend. Mostly, I wanted him to be happy, whether he believed it or not.

The bell on the door dinged as I walked in, making me smile. "I've missed that sound."

Violet stood behind the counter, wearing an apron emblazoned with the Gardner Sisters Nursery logo. "I know, me too. The old one was lost in the vandalism, so I got a new one."

I took off my coat and headed to the back room, setting it on the chair in front of my old potter's table. I guessed it was Violet's now that I'd separated the landscaping part of our business. I missed it. Working with plants and soil was my happy place. The one place where all my troubles slipped away. Maybe I needed to set one up at the landscaping office, but then I quickly realized that would probably never work. I'd worry about that later.

When I walked back out, I took in the layout of the store. The shelves had been stocked the last time I'd been in, but since then, she'd made the place homey and cheery and very festive. Valentine's Day was only five weeks away, and miniature rose bushes in white, red, and pink ceramic pots were spread through the shop.

Violet's gaze followed me. "Do you want to wear an apron too?"

"Um… yeah." It was odd to feel like a stranger in my own business. Maybe I'd purposely separated myself from the nursery just a little too well.

She handed me a black apron, and after I pulled it over my head, she grabbed the strings and tied it in the back.

"Are you excited about today?" I asked.

"Yes," she gushed. "I'm glad to be back to work. I feel like I belong here, you know?"

I turned to look at her. "I know, Vi. You do belong here… You're a natural."

Tears filled her eyes. "Thanks for not taking my dream away from me."

I wasn't sure what to say. She'd betrayed me multiple times. But she was my sister and that overruled every other consideration. "I love you, Violet. You know that. But I can't take another betrayal from you, so consider this fair warning."

"I know." She shook her head. "I'm sorry."

I pulled her into a hug. "I know you are. Let's just try to start over, okay?" I released her and pulled back, looking into her eyes. "We don't fill the same roles any more. I've grown up and you don't have to protect me anymore."

Fiery determination set her eyes ablaze. "You can't ask that of me, Rose. I'll always want to protect you. Are you saying you'd just stand by if you saw me gettin' hurt?"

"Of course not. How can you even ask?"

"You're asking me to refrain from doing that very thing."

I grabbed both of her biceps. "Violet, I think your definition of protecting me and my definition are two very different things."

She was about to answer when the front door dinged. I turned to see Neely Kate enter the store with a cake box in hand. Her face lit up when she saw us. "Am I missing somethin' good?" Neely Kate was always after me to confront Violet about her behavior.

I let my hands fall to my sides. "Of course not. Vi and I were having a heart-to-heart."

Her eyebrows lifted in amusement as she walked past us to the table Violet had set up in the back of the store. "Don't let me stop your chat."

Vi's eyes clouded and she turned and marched back to the register. "Rose, I take it you're going to make sure your employee gets the cake set up okay?"

"Sure."

Neely Kate shot me an amused look and whispered, "Is bein' called your employee instead of your friend a promotion or a demotion?"

I shook my head and grinned at her. "She's just upset that you're doin' the books now," I whispered. "She takes it personally that she's being audited. She says it makes it look like she was stealing money."

Neely Kate's mouth pressed into a thin line and she hissed, "But she *was* stealin' money!" The balanced cake began to wobble in her arms. I grabbed it and set it down on the table.

"She wasn't really stealing," I whispered in Violet's defense. "She was just misappropriating funds."

"Like that's any better," she scoffed.

"Give her a few weeks. She'll get over it."

"Hmm." She put her hands on her hips and shot an angry glare at the register.

Perhaps asking Neely Kate to help out had been a bad idea.

The bell on the door jingled again, signaling the arrival of our first customer, a woman from Jonah's church. Neely Kate cut her a piece of cake while I helped her pick out a plant to give her neighbor as a housewarming gift. As soon as she left, I got Neely Kate an apron and helped her on with it.

"You're just trying to hog-tie me here so I can't leave," she said, but something in her voice sounded off.

"Neely Kate, are you feelin' okay? You look a little pale."

She rested her hand on her stomach. "Now that you mention it, I'm a bit queasy and my back kind of aches."

"You should sit down. I'll get you a chair from the back."

"And have Violet accuse me of sitting down on the job? I don't think so."

"I'm your employer and I'm ordering you to sit."

She flashed me a grin, though it was several wattages dimmer than usual. "You're so bossy."

"I know." I grabbed a folding chair from the back room and set it up by the table, making sure Neely Kate obeyed me.

As the morning progressed, more people started to stream through the door. We were getting more customers than we'd expected, and even better, they were all buying things. Through it all, I kept on eye on Neely Kate. After she drank some water and ate a banana she had in her purse, some of the color returned to her face.

Close to noon, she stood by the cake, not looking quite right. I made my way over to her. "Maybe you should go home, Neely Kate."

"I'm fine," she said, rubbing her back. "I just slept in a weird position last night is all."

"Are you sure?"

She looked exasperated. "Stop babyin' me. I'm fine."

"If you change your mind—"

"I won't." Her gaze shifted to the door. "Who's that? I've never seen her before. I'd know if I had."

I wanted to tell Neely Kate that she didn't know everyone in Fenton County, but some days it felt like she did. I definitely didn't recognize the woman who'd just walked into the nursery. Her dark hair was bobbed with several blue streaks. She wore jeans and a khaki coat.

"I tell you what," Neely Kate said. "I think I could pull off color streaks."

I shot her a look. She'd mentioned the same thing in New Orleans when we met a woman with pink stripes in her hair. Considering how things had turned out with her, I was surprised Neely Kate hadn't changed her mind on the merits of such a hairstyle.

The woman walked into the middle of the store and Violet circled the counter to greet her. "Welcome to Gardner Sisters Nursery. Can I help you find something?"

The woman looked Violet up and down. "Are you Rose Gardner?"

Violet looked taken back. "And you are…?"

She flashed Violet a sarcastic grin. "Someone looking for Rose Gardner."

"Are you sure you don't know who that is?" Neely Kate asked me in a whisper.

"I think I'd remember her, Neely Kate." But she obviously knew me. The question was how.

Violet had taken on her familiar role of momma bear. "I'd like to know how you know her and why you're lookin' for her."

I stepped forward. "It's okay, Violet. I'll talk to her."

"Rose," Violet hissed. "I don't like her attitude."

Neither did I. She put off a cocky air, but I saw no reason not to talk to her. "It's fine. I'll see what she wants."

The bell on the door announced another customer and Violet reluctantly went to greet her.

The woman chuckled and closed the distance between us. "Rose." It was a statement.

"What can I do for you?"

She looked me up and down. "You're not what I was expecting."

I squared my shoulders. "You have me at a disadvantage. You've clearly heard about me, but I don't know anything about you."

I expected her to introduce herself, but she moved on to another topic instead. "What do you know about Hilary Wilder?"

Neely Kate tried to get around me, but I shifted to the side and blocked her path. "If you're lookin' for gossip, I suggest you get your hair done at Beulah's Nip and Clip," I said. "You'll get more than you bargain for there."

She laughed. "Really? That's all you can say about her?"

I shook my head. "I'm sorry, but I'm not gonna discuss Hilary Wilder with you."

"Why not? She's more than happy to talk about you with anyone who asks."

"What Hilary does is her business, not mine."

The woman looked perplexed. "Why aren't you with Joe?"

"Who *are* you?" Neely Kate demanded.

"An interested party."

"You can be interested all you like," I said. "But my personal life is no one's business but my own."

"I can get my answers elsewhere."

Neely Kate worked her way around me. "Then maybe you should move along to elsewhere."

The woman chuckled again and looked around the store. "I think I'll check out your merchandise first."

"Don't you even think about casin' the place," Neely Kate warned.

The woman laughed again and started to wander the floor.

Violet shot me a glance that told me she wanted to kick her out, but I saw no reason for it. Maybe she'd buy something. God knew we weren't in any position to turn away business. I'd expected curious gawkers. We were lucky we hadn't had any before this customer.

Ten minutes later she was still there, ignoring our offers of help. She just said she was waiting for the perfect gift, though the way she kept glancing at the door told me she didn't expect to find it on the shelves. A grin spread across her face when Joe walked through the door. But he looked less than thrilled to see her.

"What are you doin' here, Kate?"

Kate? His *sister* Kate? Her questions made more sense, though there was still the issue of why she was here asking them and why she was being so belligerent.

"I'm trying to get some of the answers you wouldn't give me."

Joe's face flushed with anger. "I told you to leave it alone. It's time for you to go."

She picked up a black and white, cow-shaped gravy boat. "But I haven't purchased my housewarming gift for Hilary yet."

Joe rolled his eyes. "You're stirring up a hornet's nest, Kate. I know this is your idea of fun, but it's time for you to stop."

She hugged the ceramic cow to her chest. "Now, Joe. When have you known me to back down from a challenge?"

"You are messin' with my personal life. *Stop.*"

She stepped closer to him until they were no more than a few inches apart. "I'm sorry, big brother, but I just can't do that. Now that I know we're on the same side, I plan on jumping into the ring to help you."

"How many times do I have to tell you that I don't *want* your help?"

She shrugged, her lips curling up into a smug smile. "You're getting it anyway." She spun around and set the cow on the counter in front of the register. "Do you gift wrap?"

Violet's gaze shifted to me before moving back to Kate. "Yes, but it's extra."

"I don't mind. Make sure it's classy." She scratched her chin, as if deep in thought. "Oh, wait. You *do* know what classy is here in Fenton County, don't you?"

I expected Neely Kate to pounce on her. When she didn't, I turned around to see her clutching her stomach, her eyes wide with terror. "Neely Kate?"

Her face was paler than I'd ever seen it, and I noticed a small pool of blood on the floor at her feet. "Joe!" I screamed, rushing over to my friend as she started to collapse.

He was at her side before I could even process what was happening. "Violet, call 911," he shouted.

Violet grabbed the phone and made the call as I knelt beside Joe and my best friend. He gently patted her face. "Neely Kate? Can you hear me, honey?"

Her eyes were closed and she didn't respond.

"She'd hate you callin' her honey," I said, my voice shaky from my terror.

"I know, that's why I said it." He picked up her wrist to feel for her pulse, then turned to me. "What happened?"

"I don't know." I brushed back my hair, trying to sort it all out in my head. "She said she was queasy and her back hurt. I tried to send her home, but she refused to go." My eyes darted to the blood on the floor. "She's losin' her baby, isn't she?"

"Maybe, maybe not. Let's focus on the maybe not, okay?"

I nodded. "Okay. You're right."

Violet moved behind us. "They said the ambulance has a flat tire and won't be here for a bit. Maybe twenty minutes."

"You didn't tell them it was Neely Kate, did you?" he demanded. "They'll take longer if they know it's her."

"No. I didn't tell them."

"The damn ambulance system in this county," he said in disgust, then shook his head. "We can't wait that long." He scooped her up in his arms and climbed to his feet. "I'll take her myself."

"I'm coming with you," I said, following behind him.

"I want you to, so don't expect a fight from me."

Genuine concern filled Kate's face as she ran for the door and held it open for Joe and me. "What can I do?" she asked.

He shifted Neely Kate in his arms so her head wouldn't flop backward. "I think you've done more than enough." His tone was harsh, but it softened when he addressed me. "Rose, open the back door of my car and I'll put her in. Why don't you sit back there with her?"

"Okay." I did exactly that, propping an unconscious Neely Kate so she was leaning against me.

As he shut the back door, Kate was opening the passenger door. "What the hell do you think you're doing?" Joe shouted. "Butt out of this, Kate!"

"No. I'm coming." She slid into the seat and closed the door.

Joe's face turned beet red as he got in. "I don't have time to argue with you over this, but we will be talking about this later." He took off, turning on his police lights and siren as he raced through town.

I picked up Neely Kate's hand, worried by how cold it was. "Neely Kate. You have to wake up." I fought to keep from crying.

Kate turned around and got onto her knees so she was facing us. "Keep talking to her."

My gaze shot up to her. I was about to say something snippy, but she cut me off.

"Remind her of what she's fighting for."

Kate was right, as hard it was to admit considering the first impression she'd made. "Neely Kate. Hang on, sweetie. Joe's takin' you to the hospital, so you just hang on, okay?"

Less than five minutes later the hospital came into view.

"We're here," Joe said, pulling into the hospital entrance and driving right up to the emergency room doors. He honked his horn several times, then hopped out and opened the back door, scooping Neely Kate into his arms again before anyone even came out. He barged through the electric doors, Kate and me fast behind him. "I have a twenty-four-year-old woman, eleven weeks pregnant. She passed out and is unresponsive. She needs to be seen *stat.*"

The receptionist took one look at Joe and Neely Kate and pushed a button. The doors behind his desk swung open. Joe barged through them, but when I started to follow, the receptionist glared at me. "Not you. You wait out here."

I was about to protest, but Kate grabbed my arm and gently tugged me back. "Let them do their work. Joe will tell us what's going on in a few minutes."

I looked at her, surprised by her gentle tone.

She gave me a wry smile. "I am capable of being nice. I just don't tend to show it." When I gave her a blank stare, she said, "One of the quirks of growing up as a Simmons." She pulled me over to the seating area near the receptionist's desk, helping me sit down.

My hands began to shake. "I need to call her husband, Ronnie." Tears burned my eyes. "But I don't have my phone and I don't know his number."

She put her hand on my shoulder. "It's obvious Joe cares about her too. I'm sure he'll call him. That's part of his job, after all. You've had too much of a shock to handle it."

I wondered if it would be better for Ronnie to hear the news from Joe or me, then I decided no matter who the news came from, it wouldn't be good.

"I had a friend who bled during her pregnancy and she ended up doing just fine," Kate said, patting my hand. "Six months later she gave birth to a beautiful baby boy."

I jerked my hand free. "Why are you bein' so nice to me now?"

"We got off on the wrong foot. I don't want to be your enemy. Never did."

"Then in the future, you might want to change the way you introduce yourself to people."

She chuckled. "Sorry. Habit."

I still didn't trust her, but she was the least of my worries. When my legs became steadier, I got up and began to pace, though the movement didn't help any. I was staring at the double doors behind the desk when Joe emerged from them with slumped shoulders, rubbing his eyes. I raced over to him. Drops of blood stained his uniform which only spiked my fear. "How is she?"

He took my hands. "She had an ectopic pregnancy and her fallopian tube ruptured. They're taking her into surgery now."

I shook my head. "That's impossible. She had an ultrasound a few weeks ago. They saw the baby and everything was fine!"

"Apparently, she had *two* babies. They missed the one in her fallopian tube. The doctor said they're gonna do their best to save the other one," he choked out, tears in his eyes. "But they have to save *her* first. It's bad, Rose."

"*What?*" I felt lightheaded. "But she was fine just this morning."

"They said that's how it happens. Sometimes there's no warning."

"I can't lose her, Joe. I just can't."

He tipped up my chin. "Look who you're talking about. Neely Kate is the most stubborn woman I know, and that's saying something considerin' how my life is chock full of stubborn women. She's too mule-headed to kick the bucket just yet. She's got a whole lifetime of harassment planned out for me."

I nodded, starting to cry. "Yeah, you're right."

"Then this Neely Kate sounds like someone I want to know," Kate said. She'd walked up beside us without me noticing.

Joe's body went rigid. "I think you've done enough."

Her face softened. "I just want to help, Joe. That's all I want to do."

I could tell Joe was about to put up a fight. I put my hand on his arm. "Joe, I'm fine if she stays."

He looked down at me, clenching his jaw. "You've got enough on your hands without my sister stirring up her usual shit."

"She's actually made me feel better. Don't kick her out on my account."

He stared at Kate for several long seconds, then shook his head in defeat before leading me back to the chairs.

"We need to call Ronnie," I said, panicking that we still hadn't called him.

Joe released a heavy sigh. "I already took care of it. I didn't want him driving to the hospital upset, so I had a deputy drop by his shop to tell him the news and bring him in with lights and sirens."

I started to cry. "I need to call Mason, but I don't have my phone."

He swallowed and his eyes filled with sorrow. "I already called him. He should be here any minute. I called Jonah too."

The significance of what he'd done wasn't lost on me. He wasn't a fan of Jonah and he couldn't stand Mason even more. "Thank you," I said through my tears.

He nodded and averted his gaze.

I was so scared I couldn't even think straight. "I don't know what to do. What do I do?"

"There's nothing to do but wait and pray."

I had a whole lot of bargaining to do with the man upstairs.

*****

Thirty-Four and a Half Predicaments

Available April 28, 2015

About the Author

Denise Grover Swank was born in Kansas City, Missouri and lived in the area until she was nineteen. Then she became a nomadic gypsy, living in five cities, four states and ten houses over the course of ten years before she moved back to her roots. She speaks English and smattering of Spanish and Chinese which she learned through an intensive Nick Jr. immersion period. Her hobbies include witty Facebook comments (in own her mind) and dancing in her kitchen with her children. (Quite badly if you believe her offspring.) Hidden talents include the gift of justification and the ability to drink massive amounts of caffeine and still fall asleep within two minutes. Her lack of the sense of smell allows her to perform many unspeakable tasks. She has six children and hasn't lost her sanity. Or so she leads you to believe.

You can find out more about Denise and her other books at:
www.denisegroverswank.com
or email her at denisegroverswank@gmail.com

CPSIA information can be obtained at www.ICGtesting.com
Printed in the USA
LVOW07s1939211015

459186LV00030B/1821/P